J. Lloyd Morgan

The night the Port-A-Potty burned down

and

Other Stories

Pendr Publishing
http://www.jlloydmorgan.com

ISBN-10: 0988633000
ISBN-13: 978-0-9886330-0-1

Cover by: Kelley Morgan
Edited by: Kayla Echols

For Amy, Thad and Ken, siblings who helped shaped

the way I think.

(Meaning, if you don't like this book, it's their fault.)

Introduction

Writers write because they have something to say. And often, they aren't shy about their opinions. I'm no different.

This book consists of short stories, insights, and observations. Some are humorous. Some are thought-provoking. And some are downright strange.

My goal isn't to convert anyone to my way of thinking. What *do* I want? I would like you, the reader, to laugh, think, and have emotional reactions. Heck, I even want people to disagree with me.

After all, writers aren't the only ones with something to say.

Value Perception

$19.99.

That was the price on the item. $19.99. As we stood there waiting for the friendly man at the cell phone store to program my daughter's new phone, I kept looking at the price on the protective case.

$19.99.

Somewhere in the recesses of my mind I remembered being told a story about why things were marked down a penny. (Ok, side note: there is no such thing as a U.S. penny. The official name is one cent piece—look it up if you think I'm lyin'.)

Before the days of the fancy cash registers we have today, businesses had to keep track of things by hand. By marking things down a penny, at the end of the shift, the owner (or whoever) could compare the number of things sold to how many pennies, er, one cent pieces, were gone from the cashbox.

So, if 11 things were sold, then 11 cents would be handed back to the customers. Right? In theory, it makes sense.

But then there's another concept that the human mind sees $19.99 not nearly as expensive as $20.00, which, if you think about it, is kinda weird. After all, $19.99 has a lot of 9's in it. And 9 is the highest single digit out there. Whereas $20.00 has a bunch of zeros, which is the lowest single digit, so you would think our brains would say, "Wow! That has three 9's in it, and that one has three 0's in it. The one with the 9's must be really good!" Actually, maybe pricing something at $19.99 versus $20.00 works on both levels. It lets us think that something is cheaper, yet of more worth.

Whoa, I think I blew my own mind.

Not to be outdone are the gasoline prices. That gallon of gas that is $3.59? It's actually $3.59 and 9/10ths. Talk about added value while saving us all those 1/10ths of a cent per gallon!

And there is the other side of the coin (pun intended—though even I admit it was lame). How many times have you seen the variation on the phrase "It *could* be worth *up to* $X,XXX,XXX.XX!" I'm leery about promises that contain variables. And usually the more variables, the more leery I become. In this case, "could" and "up to" are variables.

Obviously the trick here is to have the highest possible dollar amount out there for people to see. That's what they'll focus on, not the variable words.

When I got my job right out of college selling cell phones, they said we could earn up to (whatever the dollar amount was) per year. However, as we soon discovered, the only way to hit that number was to basically sell everything in the store on a daily basis. Could it be done? Possibly. And possibly a stranger may walk up to me and give me a million bucks because I'm wearing brown shoes.

In the spirit of this wonderful concept, I'm going to make an offer you can't refuse. This is 100% legit.

Here it goes:

"I could possibly, maybe, perhaps give you up to $50,000.00 in cash if you get 100 people to buy this book. Certain terms and restrictions apply.*

*In order to win, all 100 people must sign up between 3:00 am and 3:05 am, Jamaican time, on any given Tuesday. For each of the hundred people, $10 will be earned if they have a "J" in their name (it can't be the first letter). $20 will be earned for each person who was born in Wyoming. $20 will be earned for each person who is left-handed. $450 will be earned for those who have been struck by lightning— twice, while in Italy. Cash award will be dispensed in sums of 25 cents a day for the next 200,000 days. Winner forfeits any cash not awarded to them if either the winner or J. Lloyd Morgan dies before all sums can be dispersed. Contest void in any state that doesn't have an 'x' in the state name."

Good luck to all those entering the contest!

Natural Flavor

Dinner time at the Morgan household can be quite the interesting experience. Aside from talking about the day's events, we'll talk about any number of things. One thing I love to do is to "acquaint" my four young daughters with the music of the 80's. YouTube is an amazing tool for such an activity. It's something else to see your seven year old daughter do *The Safety Dance*.

There are other times when the kids will ask questions like "Why does it say 'Tomato' Ketchup? Are there other kinds?" So we'll look it up. And yes, there are other types. One we found was "Banana Ketchup." Then that leads to the question, "Why is it called 'Yellow' Mustard? Are there other kinds?" The answer? Yes. Mustard can be brown. Heck, with a little food coloring, it can be any color you want.

But we aren't content to leave things there. Next, we'll investigate the ingredients of various foods. Doing this led to a shocking and somewhat disturbing discovery: Natural Flavor. What the heck is Natural Flavor and why is it in so many different foods?

I randomly sampled items from my fridge and pantry, and these are the things that I found contained this mysterious Natural Flavor: Apple / Cranberry juice, spray butter, mixed berry yogurt, salsa, maple syrup, mayo, mustard (yellow), ketchup (tomato), animal crackers, hot cocoa mix, tomato soup, chocolate frosting, root beer, granola bars, pudding, and macaroni & cheese. Whoever invented this Natural Flavor must be a bazillionaire—I mean, it is in everything!

But as odd as Natural Flavor is, there is something even stranger: Artificial Flavor. How can flavor be artificial? After all, it has to be made from something on the Earth, right? Is it just a combo of two Natural Flavors? Does that mean if I mix chocolate and peanut butter together, I've created an Artificial Flavor? One thing I know for sure is that Natural Flavor and Artificial Flavor are not opposites. Of the items listed above, several of them had both Natural *and* Artificial Flavor. (Maple syrup, hot cocoa mix, chocolate frosting, root beer, and strangely enough, granola bars.) If they were opposites, wouldn't they just cancel each other out? Or if it was like matter and anti-matter, wouldn't having both ingredients in the same product be dangerous?

However, of all the items I sampled, there were two that were the most disquieting: hot dogs and bologna. Neither of these had Natural nor Artificial Flavor—but both of them did share a common ingredient: something simply called "Flavor." And thank goodness they did! Can you imagine how they would taste without "Flavor"?

I honestly intended to leave Natural Flavor alone after that. Really. However, it seemed that Natural Flavor wouldn't leave me alone.

The drink for dinner one night was lemonade—or something pretending to be lemonade. I'm a virtual connoisseur of lemonades (I guess that is a hobby you pick up when you don't partake of the strong drink), and this, my friends, was no lemonade.

My sweet wife tried to explain that there wasn't enough of the mix left to make real lemonade and it was actually just slightly flavored water. However, it was yellow and smelled lemony—watered down or not, it was something I needed to investigate.

To avoid getting sued, I will not reveal the brand of the alleged lemonade. But as I examined the container, a couple of things caught my attention right away.

#1: It clearly stated on the front that there were no "Artificial Flavors" in this mix.

#2: Its selling point was "Lemonade Drink Mix. Naturally Flavored with other Natural Flavor." Wait … what? "Naturally Flavored with other Natural Flavor?" What does that even mean?

So, off to the back label I went. There had to be some sort of explanation. But no! The ingredients were printed right where the lid joins with the jar—and when the lid was opened, the list of the ingredients was obliterated. How you mock me, you faux lemonade!

Hello! What's this? Below the ingredients in bold were the allergy warnings. Let's see here. This so-called lemonade may contain traces of milk, eggs, coconut, wheat, soy, and ... tilapia. Tilapia? Wasn't that some sort of fish?

Alas, if only the lemonade had traces of lemons.

Sigh.

The Night the Port-A-Potty Burned Down

I didn't know my neighbors. Not really. There was an older woman who lived across the street. The neighbors to our right were a nice couple with two kids. Aside from that, everyone else was a mystery.

We didn't have any neighbors to our left. Instead, there was a little league baseball diamond. It was actually one of the reasons we decided to buy the house in that neighborhood. Open spaces were rare in our part of Connecticut, so to be able to look out the window and see a large, green field was a special treat.

Alas, with the good also comes the bad. The field had a parking lot, and it didn't have any street lights. It seemed that every night there was a car or two parked there. Why would you park your car in a dark parking lot? Well, it isn't to read scriptures or to have a quilting bee.

Our little girls always wanted to ride their bikes or go play in the field, but before they could, I'd have to go clean up the area first. There were broken bottles that had a number and then the word "proof" written on the labels, beer cans, and other things that are frankly too disgusting to mention.

One summer, the town put a port-a-potty by the parking lot. The blue stall stood like a beacon of relief at the edge of the field. Then one night, someone (more than likely one of these ne'er-dowells that parked there at night) lit the port-a-potty on fire. I'm not exactly sure how you do that, but I will tell you that when it caught fire, it really burned. The reclusive people in our neighborhood, including us, came out to watch while the fireman let the port-a-potty burn—it was beyond saving.

For the first time since we had lived there, we shared a moment with our neighbors. We talked about how it was a shame that someone would burn down such a defenseless port-a-potty, or mentioned how humid the summer had been. Heck, for a moment there, I thought we were going to hold hands and start to sing "Kumbaya."

In the end, we all went back to our houses. That wasn't the start of neighborhood picnics or get-togethers. Yet, when we saw one of our neighbors out and about, we'd smile and wave. And to be clear, the wave wasn't the typical one you'd see in Connecticut. Oh no. When neighbors waved to us, they'd use more than one finger.

Angry Birds

It was one of those rare moments when I was home alone and my imagination was on fire. I sat in front of my computer, lost in my own little world as I worked on my next book. During times like these, I'm fairly oblivious to everything around me. Time absolutely flies, with only my grumbling stomach as a reminder I've been sitting in one place too long.

Of course, if someone calls or the doorbell rings, I'm aware enough to respond. On this day, however, it wasn't either of those things that drew me away from my writing zone. It was the sound of something banging. Usually I dismiss such sounds as the kids doing something that I probably don't want to know about, but should respond to. But then again, I was home alone.

The sound was random enough that I couldn't imagine what could be causing it. I tried to dismiss it, but it kept happening. Finally, I had to investigate. I went upstairs and looked in each room, trying to find something out of place, but found nothing.

I heard it again, and it came from downstairs. We had lived in North Carolina for over three years and were still getting used to things we hadn't experienced elsewhere, like the time I was mowing the lawn and I saw a stick on the grass ahead of me. At least I was sure it was a stick until it lifted its head and stuck its forked tongue out at me. And in that case, I did what any self-respecting man would do. I screamed like an 8-year-old girl and promptly ran the snake over with my mower. And I let it sit there a couple of minutes so I wouldn't see any trace of the slithering creature.

Thoughts like that ran through my head as I headed downstairs to investigate. I got to our main hallway and stood there, listening for it to happen again.

For a long, drawn-out moment...nothing.

Then, there it was again! The sound came from the kitchen area. Upon entering said location, I noticed a red cardinal sitting on the porch right by our sliding glass doors. I stood there for a moment and watched as the bird flew to one of the trees behind our house and perched itself on a branch. While this was odd, it didn't explain what was making the sound.

That's when the cardinal flew from the tree and right at the sliding glass doors. The bird hit the glass, creating the sound I'd been hearing, but not hard enough for it to hurt it or our window. It was one of the oddest things I'd seen.

I didn't want the bird to hurt itself, so I closed the curtains, hoping to trick the bird into thinking there was a solid object there. It seemed to have worked because I didn't hear the sound after that.

What made this whole situation somewhat surreal is that my youngest daughter and I would play a game on my cell phone called "Angry Birds." In this game, birds hurtle themselves at objects and buildings, trying to crush the evil green pigs inside that have stolen their eggs.

I'm not an evil green pig, and I haven't stolen anyone's eggs. But one of the birds in the game was a red cardinal.

Life imitating art?

To Be Honest Whichya

As I've moved around the country, I've noticed phrases or words that are common to that particular area. When we moved to Idaho, it was "whatnot." As in, "For dinner, we'll have burgers, fries and whatnot." Or also, "When you do a load of laundry, do the socks, underwear and whatnot."

Sometimes you needed to be careful how you used the term "whatnot" since it could leave quite a bit to the imagination. Need an example? Imagine asking someone out on a date. When your person of choice asks, "What are we going to do?" and you respond, "I thought we'd drive up to the mountains, look at the stars, have a good talk, kiss a little and whatnot." You could be meaning "reading scriptures"—your date could take it another way.

So, to avoid confusion, we should always be clear and honest. Right?

Which brings me to my next phrase which I picked up in Connecticut: "To be honest with you." (Or if you want to say it right, it sounds more like "To be honest whichya.")

People would say this when they wanted to make you understand they were being sincere. But why would they need to clarify this point? Doesn't using that phrase seem to indicate that most of the time the person is lying to you?

I was in a discussion where we talked about what it meant to be honest. My first comment was, "Being honest isn't the same thing as speaking whatever is on your mind." This raised a few eyebrows. But the word "honest" comes from the meaning "respectable, decent, of neat appearance." Don't believe me? Look it up.

Sometimes people confuse offering their opinion as "I'm just being honest." What's left out of this sentence is "… about what I think."

And frankly, what some people think can be pretty messed up.

Sometimes being too honest with your opinion can cause issues. Imagine getting pulled over for speeding though you didn't think you were. Let's say this police officer is particularly attractive. Would you dare say, "There is no way I was speeding. You must be bored to pull me over for something so trivial when there are so many other bad people out there breaking more serious laws. Oh, and by the way, you are smokin' hot."

And of course, there is the oldie but goodie that we men get asked time and again from our wives: "Does this dress make me look fat?" Try answering, "It's not the dress. It's your butt."

I'll bet no amount of saying, "You told me you wanted me to be honest in our marriage!" will keep you from sleeping on the couch.

Don't Let the Facts Ruin a Good Story

Have you ever told a story in a group setting when a friend or spouse or family member interrupted you and said, "That's not the way it happened!" And then they correct some minor part of the story with a "fact" that didn't really matter to the point of the story.

Here's an example: (completely fictitious, of course, to protect the innocent, namely me) I'm at a party with TV co-workers for the holidays. The subject of typos or on-air mistakes gets brought up. I start to tell the story of when we aired a tease that said, "Gigantic Monsoons Ahead!" and instead of video of stormy weather, there is video of ladies getting mammograms.

As I'm telling the story, I say, "It was about 6 months ago when we had this tease that said 'Gigantic Monsoons Ahead!' when—" I'm interrupted by a co-worker, who says, "It couldn't have been 6 months ago because I was on maternity leave and I remember that happening. It must have been more like 4 1/2 ago, because if you think about it, that would have been closer to monsoon season."

I'll stop the story there. But hopefully you get the point. Was it 6 or 4 1/2 months? Does it really matter to the point of the story?

Of course, this carries over to my work as an author. Since my first two books take place in a made-up land during a medieval time frame, I'm sure historians would go ape doo-doo over all the words in the book that wouldn't have been used in that time period. (Side note: I did take the word "OK" out of the books on my own because that's a modern term.)

However, does it really matter?

I love the saying that we must "suspend our disbelief to be entertained." To me, that doesn't mean throwing all logic out the window—like having King Arthur use a laser gun to kill Attila the Hun—but rather, ignoring little things here and there that may not be perfect, or even 100% accurate, to enjoy the overall experience.

So the next time someone is telling a story, think about the point they are making before you interrupt and say, "It wasn't really a purple dinosaur, as much as it was magenta."

Inconvenient Convenience

There are a number of new inventions and such designed to make our lives easier. More often than not, they do just that. Want to check your bank account balance at 3:17 am? No problem! They have online banking! Want to buy tickets for that movie without standing in line out in the elements? No problem! Buy and print your own tickets at home! And so on and so on.

And then there are things that are good in theory, yet...

My mom, sister, and her boyfriend flew into town one night. I had parked the car in one of those "press here to get a ticket" type garages at the airport. It turned out that their flight was on the far end of the terminal, so we figured they would stay there and I'd hoof it back to the car and then pick them up at the curb.

There were signs everywhere reminding you to take the ticket you got when you parked. Why? Because they had these automated machines inside the terminal where you could pay, get a receipt, and then when you drove out, you just inserted the receipt into another machine, and ta-da!—the gate would open for you. No waiting in line behind other cars as the people rummage through their ash tray for coins. No more having to deal with rude and indifferent employees at the toll booth. (Note: to be fair, not all workers are like that.) It's a great idea!

Unless something goes wrong with the machines.

Which is exactly what happened to me.

I inserted my ticket. It then asked me to insert my debit or credit card so it could charge me the grand total of $1.00. After I put in my card, it gave me an error message and spit out the card with such fury that it nearly cut me in two. OK, maybe I'm being a bit over dramatic about it, but still, it fired out my card pretty quickly.

I tried to put the card back, but by that time, it said "please insert ticket." I *had* inserted my ticket—it was in the machine, but I didn't have a receipt. So, after looking over the machine for options, I hit the "cancel" button. Nothin'. I tried it again. Still nothin'. Of course, there weren't any employees close by.

Hello! What's this? A small "help" button off to the side. I pressed this "help" button, in hopes of getting just that. After a moment, a voice from a speaker asked, "Do you need help?" (I almost got snippy and said, "Isn't that what the help button is for?" But I was nice.) "Yes, the machine ate my ticket." The response? A six or seven step set of instructions which resulted in me pressing the cancel button. Once I figured out that was what they were going to have me try, I explained I had already attempted that action.

They had me try it again, none-the-less, which I did. Still, no ticket. I was starting to feel like I'd have better luck finding a golden ticket in a candy bar wrapper. Finally the voice said, "We'll send someone right down."

15 minutes went by. I pushed the help button again. No answer. I pressed the cancel button again. Still nothin'. Finally, I got fed up and went to my car. I had family waiting at the other end of the terminal, after all!

I got to the gate where you were supposed to put in your receipt. Again, I lacked one of those. On the far end were two lanes that said "Assistance." So I went there. What did the less than enthusiastic worker there ask me? "Where is your receipt?"

"I don't have one."

"Where is your ticket?"

"It was eaten by the machine."

"Did you try to press the cancel button?"

"Yes. It didn't work."

"Did you try to press the help button?"

"Yes, and they said help was coming, but no one came."

She looked at me blankly. After a moment she asked, "How are you supposed to pay me if you don't have a ticket?"

I counted to 10, then to 11 just to be safe, and said, "I wasn't here long. The machine said I owed a dollar. May I please just give you the dollar so I can go get my family?"

"I'm going to have to call my supervisor."

So she shut her window, made a call, and then sat there, looking at her cash register. She didn't even look over at me. Several minutes passed and then a man walked out of a side building and over to me.

"Where's your ticket?" he asked me.

Through gritted teeth, I told him.

"Hmmm. Did you try hitting the cancel button?" he asked.

(I'm going to edit out my response to keep you from thinking bad things of me.)

In the end, they got the maintenance man to open the machine, remove my ticket, and drive it out to me at the gate.

While we waited, they had me back up to allow them to "assist" other people.

When I finally gave the ticket to the worker, she said, "That will be $2.00."

"$2.00? No, it should only be $1.00."

Again, I got the blank look when she answered, "But you got your ticket over an hour ago, so now it's $2.00."

(Yeah, I'm going to edit out this too.)

I finally was allowed to pay my $1.00 so I could leave. As I drove out, there was a sign that read, "Paying for parking is now more convenient than ever!"

Ohmyhecknoway!

Utah Valley has its own unique culture—which isn't a bad thing. It is what it is. As a general rule of thumb, traditional swearing was frowned upon by the general public, but that didn't stop people from uttering different words instead.

What kind of "curse" words would you hear in Utah Valley when I was growing up? Well, there were "shoot," "darn," "fetch," "heck," and "jeeze," to name a few. One of the more common exclamations was "Oh my heck, no way!" However, it was so common, and often said very quickly, it was jokingly referred to as one word, hence, "ohmyhecknoway!"

There were those who told me that saying a substitute for a word was just as bad as saying the "real" swear word. For example, if I were to hit my thumb with a hammer and then proceeded to yell, "FETCH!" it was the same as dropping the F-bomb (that's a nice way we referred to that other "F" word).

On this point, I'm going to respectfully disagree. I don't believe that using a different word in place of a swear word is the same. Why? Simple. Words have power.

Now, I'm not talking about the "My name is a killing word" (*Dune* reference) type of power. I'm saying that certain words in and of themselves have power. For example: "I now pronounce you man and wife" has a totally different meaning than "I now pronounce you man and banana."

Need another example? How about instead of "You are under arrest" you say, "You are under a mattress." Still not convinced? All right, one more: instead of "You're fired!" you say, "You're hired!"

Be Good, or Be Good At It

"Be good, or be good at it" is probably not the best advice to give someone—at least to someone who you actually care about and want to be a decent person. What's another saying about advice? "Free advice is usually worth what you pay for it."

I've actually gotten a lot of good advice over the years. Some that come to mind are "don't chew tinfoil," "never spit into the wind," and "never fall asleep with gum in your mouth (it usually ends up in your hair)."

Then there are the immortal words you learn while in boy scouts. If we ever got a cut or a scrape, we were advised to "rub a little dirt on it—you'll be fine." For a twisted ankle or knee? It was always, "walk it off—you'll be fine." If the hot dog you were cooking on the end of a stick falls to the ground? "Rub the dirt off of it—you'll be fine." If you get caught in an avalanche? "Swim with the snow, and once you get buried alive, spit so you can tell which way is up, then start to claw your way out." Thank goodness I never had to test the last one to see if it worked.

Fortune cookies are very generous with advice. Here are some that I remember: "Speak when you are angry and you will make the best speech you will ever regret." "Eat your vegetables and you will grow up to be strong like Popeye." "The greatest danger could be your stupidity." "Never forget a friend, especially if he owes you money." And my favorite of all time: "Ignore previous cookie."

Another bit of advice along those lines is: "Never judge a man until you have walked a mile in his shoes. Then, when you judge him, you will be a mile away—and you'll have his shoes."

One of the best bits of advice was from my parents-in-law when my wife and I were married. In our wedding card from them, in big, underlined letters, was one word: "COMMUNICATE!" At the time, I thought, *Well, duh! Of course we'll talk to each other*. After over twenty-one years of marriage, I've truly come to understand what that means.

My wife and I are different. I know how shocking that may seem. Granted, we have a lot in common, but we are also different in a lot of ways. One thing we've become especially good at is communicating effectively. Often, that results in me saying "Yes, dear" a lot.

What we have learned is that the way one of us does or would do something may not be the only way, or even the best way. It's amazing how much I've learned by keeping my lips from flapping and opening my ears and heart to what my wife is saying.

The last bit of advice I'm going to share is one of the worst pieces of advice I have ever received.

I've held management or supervisory positions at my places of employment for a good part of the last 20 years. When I was hired at one of my jobs, my boss told me his key to successful leadership: "You have to make your employees fear you. They have to feel like their job is always at risk unless they do as they are told. Only then will you be successful."

My response? "With all due respect, I've never seen that type of behavior be effective in the long run. I believe that you should teach people what is expected of them, make sure they know how to do it, and if they can't or *won't* do it, be clear about the consequences of their actions."

He laughed and said, "Good luck with that!"

By the time I left that position, we had a solid team that worked together well and produced outstanding results. People told me what an amazing job I had done with the department. When asked, "What was the key to your success?" I responded, "Ignore previous cookie."

Do You Wanna Go Out?

Asking a person out on a date was an art form in the 80's. Granted, it still may be somewhat the same these days, but since I've not asked anyone out on a date (aside from my wife) in over 20 years, I may be a bit out of touch.

Where I grew up in Utah, we would have these "Dinner / Dances" held every 6 weeks or so. They consisted of some of the traditional themes like Homecoming, Sadie Hawkins, Junior Prom, Preference, and a few others they added along the way. You would take your date to dinner, and then go to a dance afterward.

For each of these dances, it was either boys' or girls' choice to ask. It wasn't enough to call someone up and ask, "Do you wanna go out?" Oh no. That didn't work at all. It was expected that you ask the person out in a clever way.

Sometimes you would ask by giving them instructions on how to respond. I remember for one of my dances, my then girlfriend asked me out by giving me a box of Froot Loops and some string. I was to create a necklace out of the Froot Loops in a certain pattern if the answer was "yes" and wear it to school the next day. Granted, on this one, I cheated a little. I did, in fact, create said necklace, but wore a jacket to cover it up so I wouldn't walk around the school embarrassed all day.

Then there were those times you were asked out and your response was left open. A good friend of mine had a girl respond to his request by giving him a block of ice with the response in the middle of it. After he smashed it open and got the note out, it said, "Now that we've broken the ice, I would love to go!" (Ahhhh … sweet!)

I once responded by doing the following: I bought about 30 helium balloons. On each balloon, I wrote one word of my response, with the last balloon giving the answer. I then tied the end of each string to the knot of the previous balloon. The end result was a string of balloons that reached pretty high into the sky. I then tied the bottom balloon to her door handle, rang her doorbell, and took off. She was forced to pull in the balloons one by one to read the answer (which, of course, was "yes!").

One of the crueler ways I asked someone was to get "revenge" on my girlfriend for the Froot Loop caper. I wrote my request to ask her out on 20 or so papers, about an inch square, with one word and a number so she could tell the sequence. I then crinkled up these papers. My next move? I bought a BIG old bag of popcorn—one of those about a foot in diameter and several feet long. Inside this bag, I randomly placed the papers—which happened to look very much like popcorn. (She still said yes.)

But the greatest "asking out" story is something of a legend. There was a guy who would be considered a nerd, but a very smart one who really didn't care what others thought of him. The dance was around Easter time. This guy bought a dozen or so very cheap Easter Baskets. He then wrote a note in each basket saying, "Will you go to the dance with me? If yes, answer me any way you would like. If no, please understand the sorrow this will bring me, and return the basket filled with all sorts of candy to help soothe my pain." He then gave these baskets to all the cheerleaders or girls he knew had steady boyfriends.

Not one of them said yes—but that wasn't the point. He made out like a bandit on the amount of candy he got in return.

There Are No Absolutes

One of the most frustrating classes I took in college was media ethics. The name in itself almost seems to be an oxymoron. Consider this: I went to a school that could be considered one of the most conservative universities in the nation. It had a highly regarded television program, and was fairly competitive. Those looking from afar might wonder why a school like BYU would spend so much time and money on a program designed to put people in the media workforce. My take? Media in and of itself isn't bad, just like the internet or the printing press aren't bad. However, there are those who can, and do, use it for purposes that are less than noble. The goal from the school's point of view was to get people into the media who would use it for good.

In this media ethics class, we discussed all sorts of different situations and what we would do. For example, the question was brought up, "Would you publish, or announce, the name of someone who was raped?" My gut feeling was "no." That person had been through enough without having their name put out there for everyone to know. However, there were arguments for it. Granted, at this moment I don't recall what they were, because my answer would still be "no."

The teacher of the class was a master in the art of debating. He would ask a question to the class, expect people to voice their opinion, and then he would take on the other side and tear them to shreds. Hence, the reason it was very frustrating.

It didn't take long for me to pick up on one of his tricks. Whenever someone would state their opinion in the form of a generality, for example, "people should always wear seat belts," he would counter it with a specific, "I know of a friend who wasn't wearing a seat belt, and when he got in an accident, he was thrown from the car. If he'd had his seatbelt on, he would have been crushed to death."

The teacher would also do the opposite. If you stated your opinion as a specific, for example, "My wife got married when she was 19, and we've been happily married for over 20 years," he would counter with a generality: "89% of women who get married at 19 end up divorced." (I'm just making up that stat—I have no idea what the actual number is, nor do I care.)

So how do you argue with someone who has spent a good chunk of his life debating ethical issues? For me, the answer is you *don't*. In other words, I have strong core beliefs that guide my actions on a moment by moment basis. I've developed these beliefs over the course of my life. I try to keep an open mind about certain things, and I go by the principle of "live and let live." If someone is going to try to convince me to change a core belief, they will have a difficult time doing so.

At the end of this media ethics class, the teacher said he wanted us to see that things were never black or white. There were many of shades of gray in everything. His final statement was, "There are no absolutes"—to which I responded, "Not even that one?"

Click, Click, Click

The clock radio was old. It was so old, the numbers displaying the time were on little flat plates that would flip over when the time changed. In addition, the clock made an audible clicking sound when the time changed. At night, the time could be seen by the little light that illuminated the block numbers.

It was the only clock we had in the bedroom I shared with my two brothers. It sat on a bookshelf where we could all see it. Most of the time, I wasn't aware of the little clicking sound it made—it was just background noise, like the humming of the fridge or the sound of the heated air blowing through the vents. However, on this particular night, I was very aware of the clicking sound. With each of the small, timely noises, it meant it was that much closer to morning.

I had fallen asleep fairly easily that night, but my little 8-year-old body was just too excited to stay asleep. It was with dismay that I woke up and saw that the clock read 2:30 am. Let's see. If I was to get up at 7:00 am, that meant I had, wait—let me think about it—about 4 and a half hours to go. How many clicks was that? Ug, too many to figure out.

How did I sleep most of the time? What was the trick? Certainly my body was tired enough to sleep, but my mind had other ideas. It was filled with, oh, what was that saying? Ah, yes. "Visions of sugarplums dancing in my head." (What the heck is a sugarplum anyway, and why would it be dancing? Frankly, that's kind of scary—no wonder I had a hard time sleeping if my mind was filled with visions of those.)

I didn't want to wake up my brothers. No, let them sleep. Just because I was too excited to sleep, I shouldn't deprive them of the pleasure. Dang, only 2:47 now.

"Thad? Are you awake?"

"No, and neither are you. Go back to sleep."

Harrumph.

Click, click, click. The minutes painfully passed. Click, click, click. Was that what the author was referring to when Santa came down the chimney? It kind of made sense now that I thought about it.

Then I got an idea. They said that counting sheep helped you fall asleep. But why sheep? Why not goats, or cows, or platypuses (or should platypi be the plural of platypus?) Bah, it didn't matter. Sheep were fine. I imagined 60 sheep in a pen. Each second, one sheep would jump out of the pen. I'd start the count when I heard a click of the clock. That way, when the pen was emptied, another precious minute would have passed, bringing me closer to 7:00 am.

The pen kept filling up with sheep.

"Kenny, are you awake?"

"Yes!"

"Me too!"

"I'm too excited to sleep!"

"Me too!"

Pause

Pause

Okay, back to the sheep. I waited for the clicking so the pen would fill up. Click.

Ah, there we go.

After the longest night of my life, we closed in on 7:00 am. Even Thad was awake now. We got dressed as the time got closer.

Then, it happened! 7:00 am! Whoo hoo!

"Mom! Amy! Time to get up!"

They were slow to respond. Bah! 7:02 now!

Amy came out of her room. As the oldest, and the only girl, I wondered if she understood how important this was.

"Mom's going to be taking pictures. I always look gross. I'm going to take a shower first," she said.

Are you kidding me? It was now 7:04 am! Taking a shower? I didn't think so. Thankfully my two brothers voiced their displeasure as well.

Mom was up now. "Get in a line at the top of the stairs. Youngest to oldest," she instructed.

We did as we were told. C'mon! It had to be at least 7:06 by now!

"Okay," she said. "Let's see what Santa brought."

Where Does the White Go When the Snow Melts?

I've seen snow in various amounts at different locations in my life. Unlike the common saying that Eskimos have something like 5,627 different words for snow, I just have the one—and it's a four-letter word.

Actually, that isn't fair. I have a love / hate relationship with snow. In Utah, there were days I would wake up, get ready for work or school, and then leave the house just to find my car buried under several feet of snow. Heck, I even kept a shovel in my trunk. In addition, I'd put big, heavy bags of rock salt in the trunk as well, not only to help weigh down the back of the rear-wheeled drive vehicle, but also to use as a melting agent if I got really stuck.

Even earlier in my life was the time we had a paper route. The Sunday edition was done first thing in the morning. On would go the heavy coat, mittens, two pairs of pants, and those awesome moonboots we had back in the 80's. (Actually, I sort of miss my moonboots.) I'd walk from house to house, trudging my way through snow, trying to keep the papers dry and myself warm.

Of course, this would be a good time to mention how I had to walk to school in the snow, uphill (both ways), wearing cardboard shoes, with wolves at my heels and only a "brick" of Shredded Wheat for breakfast—but it wouldn't be true. I didn't have cardboard shoes—I had my awesome moonboots.

In all my years of school in Utah, I only recall school being closed down early once. It was the day before Christmas break, and it had been snowing for several days. There was something like 5 feet of snow, and it was still coming down—hard. They let us walk home early from school that day—though it was uphill with wolves on our heels.

The most snow I've ever seen was a trip we took as scouts to Yellowstone. They said they had 12 feet of snow or something like that. The only way to get around was on snowmobiles. That was pretty sweet.

And then there came my time in Connecticut. This is where the hate part comes in. Maybe hate is too strong a word—how about "an incredibly intense dislike" for snow. Why? Because working at a TV station meant never ending snow coverage. Forget any plans you had with your family—snow meant long hours at work, telling people over and over again: "It's snowing!"

After I moved to North Carolina, snow returned to something of a wonder. One night, we got about 6 inches of snow. They said it was the first white Christmas time in the Raleigh area in 60 years. To put into perspective how much 6 inches of snow is for that part of the country, I came up with a formula:

You take the number of inches of snow, multiply it by 5, and replace the word "inches" with "feet."

Finally, there is the question of "where does the white go when the snow melts?" I've asked this question many times to many people. I've gotten all sorts of answers—some very scientific in nature. My favorite response by far was, "It goes into the ground and turns green."

Acceptable Graffiti

Mountain View High School in Orem, Utah was built while I was growing up. Rumor has it that it was built backwards—meaning the north part of the building ended up on the south side and vice-versa. Whether this is true or not, it still makes for a good story. One possible reason people think this rumor is true is because the gym, a huge, white cubed structure, was built next to one of the busiest streets in Orem.

I remember thinking, "Wow. That's not very smart. It's just begging to have graffiti sprayed on the side of it." Sure enough, not long afterwards, it happened. Several times, in fact. Eventually someone planted trees or tall shrubs around the base of the building to prevent it. I don't recall what was written on the side of the gym. It was probably "MV sucks!" or "Mountain Pew!" or something equally as lame.

I went to the other high school at the time. It was cleverly named "Orem High." One morning when arriving at school, we discovered someone had written on the side of one of our buildings in spray-paint, "To smart to live. To scared to die." Of course, the school paper took a picture of it with the caption "Too dumb to spell."

I've never understood the whole graffiti thing. Well, maybe I do—a little. After all, I write books and stories to leave my mark on the world. I just don't do it on someone else's property.

One of the things I noticed when I moved to North Carolina from Connecticut was that there wasn't graffiti on the stop signs in North Carolina. Someone said that gangs marked stop signs in Connecticut to show they "owned" that area.

I think most sensible people agree that graffiti is an eyesore—and it cheapens the look of anything it is on. Yet, as I drive around my nice little town in North Carolina, I see graffiti everywhere! People who live here may disagree until I point it out. It's not on the stop signs. It's not on the buildings. It's not under the overpasses. Where is it then?

On the ground!

Heck, there is even some on my property.

Let me explain: One year we had grass put in after I unsuccessfully tried to reseed the lawn myself (that's a story for another time). Before we could get our old lawn ripped out, some official person had to mark where the water, gas, electric and whatever else lines were under the ground. How did they do it? Spray paint! On my curb, there is still a blue line.

And that's not all. Almost every street you drive down has these markers for some reason or another. I'm not arguing that they shouldn't be marking these different utility lines so they don't get dug up, but isn't there a better way than using paint that lasts for years?

Love and Spam

Growing up in the 80's, there was a plethora of "hair bands" or "heavy metal" rock bands. It seemed that the bands had a competition to pick the scariest or most dangerous names they could think of. Example of a dangerous name? *Poison*. Then there was *Mötley Crüe*, *Slayer*, *Iron Maiden*, *Anthrax*, *Venom*, *Dark Angel*, (I'm not making these up) *Possessed*, *Motorhead*, *Nitro*, *Slaughter*, *Extreme*, *Thunder*, *T. N.T.*, *The Scream*, and *Hurricane*. The most dangerous name of all? That would have to be *Danger Danger*. You can tell they are dangerous because they used the word "danger" twice in their name. If only they had been bold enough to go with *Danger Danger Danger*.

If you couldn't think of a dangerous name, (and who could after all the good ones were taken as noted above) you could always go with naming your band after an animal. That brought us *Whitesnake*, *Scorpions*, *W.A.S.P.*, *Ratt* (spelling didn't matter), *King Kobra* (not to be confused with *Cobra*), *White Lion*, *Faster Pussycat*, *Jackyl*, and of course: *Def Leppard*. Pretty scary, eh? An animal with a hearing disability.

Then there were those that tried to sound cool, but didn't quite hit the mark. *Twisted Sister* (Okay, maybe twisted, but still a girl!), *Quiet Riot* (The sound of mute discontents roaming the streets), *Guns*

'n Roses (Ah, how sweet, you brought me roses…
and guns?), *Killer Dwarfs* (insert your own joke
here), *Y & T* (because those letters are much more
dangerous than X & Q) and *Kix*. (Finally! A heavy
metal band that is kid tested, mother approved!)

Being the smart aleck I am, while working in
the meat department of a grocery store when I was
younger, I would pass the time by making up names
for bands. I came up with the best one ever—it was
the most ridiculous name I could think of. My fellow
co-workers loved it too and so we would joke about it
anytime a customer came in wearing a T-shirt from
one of the bands mentioned above. Then one day, a
customer came in wearing a T-shirt that bore the
name of my made-up group. At the time, I couldn't
believe it. But then, it was only a matter of time
before someone would use the name *Megadeth* (yes,
to make it even cooler, they left out the "a" in death).

With that joke taken away from me, I turned
to something I thought was sillier: Spam. Back then,
Spam was only mystery meat—it wasn't used to
describe unwanted emails. Spam is inherently
funny—no doubt due to a certain comedy sketch by
Monty Python.

So what do you do with a funny word?
Simple: you replace the word "love" in all the song
titles you can think of with the word "Spam."

Imagine the following:

"I Will Always Spam You"—*Whitney Houston*
"Lost in Spam"—*Air Supply*
"Endless Spam"—*Diana Ross & Lionel Richie*
"Tainted Spam"—*Soft Cell*
"Addicted to Spam"—*Robert Palmer*
"Can't Help Falling in Spam"—*UB40*
"Crazy Little Thing Called Spam"—*Queen*
"Greatest Spam of All"—*Whitney Houston* (again)

And of course, the one that sums it all up:
"I Want to Know What Spam Is"—*Foreigner*

Be careful what you ask *Foreigner*.

The Case of the Missing Pens

"Boss, we're outta pens," Stacey said after entering my office.

I rubbed my temples. "Again? Didn't I just give you a new box?"

She shrugged. "It was a while ago—maybe last week."

I reached into one of my desk drawers and pulled out my last box of pens. "Doesn't it bother you that pens keep disappearing? Where are they going?"

"Maybe the same place all my missing socks go when I do the laundry," Stacey said. She sat down on a chair across from my desk. "Or maybe they grow little legs and run away."

I rolled my eyes. "Where would they run away to?"

"Maybe a hole in the space / time continuum has opened up in the control room," she said.

I placed the pens on the desk in front of me. As the operations manager of a TV station, I was in charge of a lot of things, one of them being supplies. And one thing my directors needed was pens to mark their scripts. Out of all the things I was in charge of, it seemed that little things, like running out of pens, tended to fill up my day. It was frustrating. These pens had to be going somewhere...

"I have an idea," I told Stacey.

She had busied herself by looking over the schedule for the following week. Without looking up, she asked, "What's that?"

"I'm tired of the directors losing pens. We're going to find out where they're running off to," I said.

She looked at me as if I had announced that we were going on a hike to find Bigfoot.

"Trust me, this will work," I said. I reached into another drawer and pulled out a roll of red gaffer's tape. It was like duct tape, only red and designed to be used in TV studios. "Help me rip off little strips of the tape. Then, we'll wrap one around the end of each pen."

Her eyebrows lifted up in interest. "Kinda like a poor man's GPS?"

"Yeah, something like that."

After several moments of work, Stacey left with a box of pens, each marked with red tape.

Over the next several days, the pens slowly began to disappear. I would check on them each time I directed the noon newscast, which I did frequently to keep up my directing skills. As each pen disappeared, I became more frustrated with my team.

I looked under work stations, in garbage cans, and even in the newsroom to see if any of the reporters, anchors, or producers had taken them.

Nada, zip, nothing.

After one particularly challenging newscast where the producer kept moving stories around, my mind was still racing. Like I always did after the noon newscast, I left to go to lunch. I noticed that it was the first sunny day we'd had in weeks; such was winter in New England.

I got into my car. I started it and turned on the music almost out of habit. Since it was sunny, I went to put on my sunglasses, but was stopped by a pen that was resting behind one of my ears. Still thinking about the newscast I had just directed, I removed the pen and went to put it into the glove compartment. I wouldn't have given it a second thought, but then I noticed that the pen had red tape on the end of it. I paused at that, and then opened the glove compartment to discover that it was full of pens—a lot of them with red tape on their ends.

Failure to Communicate—Impossible?

In the 1967 film *Cool Hand Luke*, there is a famous line: "What we've got here is a failure to communicate." I've never seen the movie, so I can't really say what was so important about the line that made it fairly well known.

What I *do* know is that the line is flawed. *GASP!*

I earned my degree at Brigham Young University in Communications—Broadcasting with an Emphasis on Production and a minor in English, so I learned a little bit about the concept of communicating.

The correct line should be, "What we have here is a failure to communicate *effectively*." Now, it may seem like I'm splitting hairs, but I'm not. As the saying goes, it makes the assumption that it is possible to not communicate at all. How would you do that?

Think about it: If I come home from work and ignore my family and say nothing to my wife, am I failing to communicate? No way! Just the opposite.

The concept here is that communication isn't solely verbal. I have learned over time that if I'm being stubborn, or I really have no interest in what is going on, I'll slump in my chair and fold my arms.

I had a boss who picked up on that and would call me out on it—which actually was a good thing because then we could discuss why I was being stubborn or disinterested.

If you still haven't bought into the concept that communication doesn't have to be verbal, next time you get into trouble—let's say you get pulled over by the police for speeding—stick your tongue out at the officer and see how well that goes over.

I would say we are always communicating, even if we are not saying anything. The trick is to communicate effectively—which can be both verbally or non-verbally.

As a final example, here is a famous baseball story (the best I can recall it). When playing in the outfield, and a ball is hit to where two of the outfielders both have a chance to catch it, it's the center fielder's job to call whether or not he can get it.

So there is this baseball player who was traded to a new team, and he plays centerfield. On the first day, a ball is hit to where both the center fielder and the right fielder can catch it. The center fielder yells, "I got it! I got it!" However, the right fielder crashes into him and the ball drops. When they get back to the dugout, the manager listens to what happened and says, "The right fielder doesn't speak English. You need to yell, 'Yo lo tango!' next time. It means, 'I got it' in Spanish."

So the next day comes and there is another game. Again, a ball is hit to where both the center fielder and the right fielder can catch it. The center fielder yells, "Yo lo tango! Yo lo tango!" Then BOOM! The center fielder and the right fielder crash into each other and the ball drops again. The center fielder is mad—until he remembers that a different player is in right field today—and he doesn't speak Spanish.

Happy Tobacco Days!

I once had to get my car safety inspected. To do so, I went to a local shop that looked to have been around forever. Though there were only a few cars in the parking lot, the lobby was fairly full. I was greeted warmly and gave my keys and registration to the man at the desk.

"It won't be long—don't you worry none; most these folks are just here to shoot the bull."

"Yup," another man said. He was old and had very few teeth in his mouth. "When you git to be our age, not much else to do but sit around and talk."

I smiled at them and took a seat.

"So, as I was telling you, Tommy," the nearly toothless man said, "Billy Bob was gettin' tired of that woodpecker waking him up in the morning. So, one day he got fed up and took his shotgun to the bird. He unloaded but didn't hit a feather. His old lady came screamin' out of the house. 'Billy Bob! What in tarnation are you doin'? You can't shoot a gun in town!' She then saw all the holes in the house caused by the buckshot. Billy Bob knew he was in trouble, so 'fore she could say anything, he said, 'I had to do somethin'! Look at all the holes the woodpecker has made in the house!'"

I couldn't help myself; I started laughing.

"What's so funny?" Tommy, the man behind the counter, asked.

I shrugged. "It was a funny story."

"It was, wasn't it?" Tommy then looked me over. "You're not from around here, are ya?"

"I've lived all over the country. I moved here about four years ago."

The nearly toothless man mumbled something under his breath about how all these Yankees were ruining things.

"Now, now there, Smoky," Tommy said to the older man. "This fella ain't done nothin' wrong."

Smoky folded his arms and grunted.

"Don'tcha mind him none," Tommy said. "Ol' Smoky is holdin' a grudge over Tobacco Days."

"Tobacco Days?" I asked.

"See!" Smoky flailed his arms in disgust. "He's not even heard about 'em!"

Tommy nodded. "Well, why don't you fill him in?"

I waited a moment while Smoky seemed to size me up. He then said, "Ever since my Grandpappy was knee-high to a tree frog, the town celebrated Tobacco Days. We'd hold it in the middle of July. Folks from all over would come to town. All the events were down there at the Masonic Temple Racetrack Park. There'd be a rummage sale, a car show, tobacco plant judgin', and at night, we'd have live music! It was the biggest event of the year. Ya couldn't go nowhere without someone smiling and wishing you a 'Happy Tobacco Days!'"

Smoky started into a fit of coughs before he continued. "It was a wonder to see. There was banners hangin' from every store front. People would decorate their houses. You couldn't go nowhere without seeing something about Tobacco Days."

"What happened?" I asked.

"What happened?" Smoky repeated. "Well, whatcha think happened? We started having all sorts of people move in from up north who looked down their noses at us. Lots of them were shop owners and refused to put up signs for Tobacco Days. Over time, people from different counties would stop comin' because they didn't feel welcomed no more. It got so bad, if you wished anyone a 'Happy Tobacco Days!' they'd give you the stink eye."

"So, about what, a dozen or so years ago, we stopped having Tobacco Days," Tommy said.

"And it's a terrible shame, too!" Smoky said. "Just because some people don't want to celebrate it, why did they have to ruin it for the rest of us?"

"Mr. Morgan, your car's done," said a man wearing a work shirt that was covered in oil and grease. "It passed."

I paid Tommy for the inspection and went to leave. For the first time, I noticed a small Christmas tree in the corner of the waiting room. After opening the door, I turned back around.

"Merry Christmas, everyone!" I said.

Everyone wished me a Merry Christmas in return, including Smoky.

I caught the eye of the nearly toothless man. I said to him, "And Smoky, in case I don't see you in July, Happy Tobacco Days!"

A x E = R (Huh?)

The end. The bottom line. The conclusion. The outcome. The result. No matter how it is stated, when it comes to judging if something is successful, we tend to look at the result. What was the final score of the game? How much money was made last month? What grades did you get on your report card? How much weight did you lose? Everywhere you look, people are focusing on the result.

In one of my previous jobs, we were taught the principle of "A x E = R." At first glance, it may look like it is a reference to someone who cuts down trees. What it means is "Actions (times) Effectiveness (equals) Results"—something I fully believe in.

After all, how do we get results? By doing something and doing it at some level of effectiveness. For example, let's look at weight loss. I think if you talk to anyone who has lost a significant amount of weight, they will tell you what they did to lose it. Maybe they started exercising thirty minutes a day. Maybe they cut out all sugars from their diet. Maybe they did a combo of both. The point is they *did* something.

But doing something isn't enough. It has to be effective. I could say, "From now on, I'm going to drink only water with my meals—and I expect to lose twenty-five pounds in a month's time."

Clearly I'm doing something, but I doubt it will be effective enough to get the results I want.

All of this may seem like common sense, and frankly, that's because it is. So why do I bring it up? Because I think that too often people look at the formula backwards.

Let me demonstrate with the weight loss example. If I were to say, "I'm going to lose five pounds this week," and then every three hours I weighed myself, I would be spending too much time on the results and not on the actions that will bring those results.

The main focus should be on the actions and their effectiveness. The results should be used as a measuring guide for how you are doing with your effective actions.

I honestly believe looking at it this way is rather encouraging. Why? Because you can control your actions. You have the power to eat that extra doughnut or not. You have the power to study that extra hour for that test.

Too often, I would get calls from my boss asking me, "What are your commitments for the day?" These "commitments" he wanted were in the form of results. Let me state this loud and clear: ***I do not believe you can commit to results.*** You can commit to effective actions—on things you can control.

If you do that, the desired results will come.

Who Says Daydreaming is a Bad Thing?

Growing up, I would daydream—a lot. Sitting in class, I'd look out the window and see something that would spark my imagination, and off I would go on some adventure. There is probably some sort of medical term for that now. And it would have to be an acronym. The medical people love their abbreviations and acronyms. I guess I would be diagnosed with having DREAM syndrome (because the word "syndrome" makes it sound really official). What would DREAM stand for? Well, let's see. How about Dysfunctional Recognition Edification Activity Murkiness? Or perhaps Dude Redirects Every Attention Much. Maybe even Doesn't Really Eat Apple Mush.

Regardless, I loved to make up adventures. My first real attempt to do so was in the 4th grade where I wrote a short story about how my friends and I were captured by aliens and I went about saving them. My real life friends liked the story so much, we went on to write twelve more short stories together which we titled *The Chronicles of Space Adventure* (or COSA if a medical person got a hold of the title).

However, I ran into a bit of a snag when it came to writing. I have a mild form of dyslexia. One way it manifests itself is in spelling, which was (and is) a mystery to me. And for better or worse, English classes often included spelling tests as part of their grading system, so you can only imagine what kind of grades I earned.

It wasn't until I took a required creative writing class in college my sophomore year that I even thought I had the ability to use my imagination to create written stories. After being told by several of my English teachers that I really should pursue something in the science fields, I had a teacher who saw something else in me. Our final project was to re-write a well-known short story of our choice from a different point of view. I chose *The Lottery*. When I got my version returned to me, it had a perfect score—something the teacher rarely awarded students. (Note: spell check is your friend—something I didn't have in high school.) He told me I had a gift. It's amazing how one person can make such a difference in your life.

Free Hugs

Has anyone ever told you, "You look like you could use a hug"? What inspires them to make such a statement? From my observations, it's because you look like you need to be cheered up. And what seemingly simple act can do that? A hug!

One day, I took my youngest daughter to a local mall for some "Daddy-Daughter" time. When we were leaving, out of the corner of my eye, I noticed two young ladies holding up signs. Usually when someone is standing outside a store with a sign it will say such things like, "Hungry and Unemployed." or "U.S. Vet. Hungry. Please Help. God Bless." or "Will work for Food." Imagine my surprise when instead these signs read, "Free Hugs."

I literally did a double take. After reading the signs again, I looked up at the two lovely young ladies. They both smiled at me. I didn't sense any malice or deception on their behalf. However, after living in Connecticut for seven years, I was quite guarded when it came to dealing with strangers. I smiled back at them and said something like, "Maybe next time" and then headed to my car with my daughter.

Yet, when I got in my car, my sense of curiosity got the better of me. Perhaps that's an occupational hazard of being an author. I had to see why these ladies were doing what they were doing.

My youngest daughter held onto my hand tightly as we re-approached the givers of free hugs.

I asked, "Okay, you've got my attention. What's up with the signs?"

One of the girls introduced herself as Genevieve, and the other was Emily. As we chatted, I discovered that they were roommates at Meredith College—a private all women's college in the area. Genevieve explained that she had a list of things she wanted to do, like a bucket list of sorts, and one of them was to offer free hugs to strangers.

My curiosity increased.

I asked them what kind of reaction they had been getting. They said mainly strange looks, though they did have a few takers.

Trying not to sound rude, I asked, "What do you hope to gain from doing this?"

The response was priceless. Genevieve said that she hoped to help people have a better day—to make the world a bit happier. Emily admitted she wasn't much of a hugger, but she was there to support her friend.

In the end, they gave hugs to my nine-year-old daughter. I didn't hug them—I guess I was still too cautious from living in Connecticut—but they achieved their mission. My day was much better for seeing their selfless act of kindness.

The Forgotten Time Zone

My first job in TV was at this wonderful station in Twin Falls, Idaho called KMVT. I primarily directed newscasts, but to fill in the rest of my work week, I worked in something called "Master Control." Sounds almost like a Sci-Fi computer villain, doesn't it?

In "Master" as we called it, we made sure the programs and commercials ran when they should. In addition, we recorded programs sent via satellite that we would play back at different times. Most of these were syndicated programs.

Idaho is in the Mountain Time zone—or as I like to call it, "the zone that time forgot." I once read an article that asked the question, "If a tree falls in the Mountain Time zone, does it make a sound?"

Case in point: you know how primetime starts 8 / 7 central? Here is why: the networks send out their primetime programs from the east coast starting at 8:00 pm. Well, primetime in the central time zone starts at 7:00 pm. Using this logic, primetime would be 6:00 pm in the mountain time zone and 5:00 pm on the west coast—but is it? Nope!

The networks send a second feed at 7:00 pm pacific time so that primetime starts at 7:00 for the west coast. But what about the Mountain Time zone? Well, we had to record the programs from the east coast and play them back an hour later.

An unscrupulous person could use this power for evil and make bets with his friends on who won *Survivor* or the Miss America title—at least until his friends caught on. (Not that I would have done that.)

One night I went into Master and was told we had missed a feed for *Home Improvement*. So I looked up who had sent the feed and saw it came from Cincinnati. 99% of the feeds came from New York, so I was a bit perplexed. I called the operator in Cincinnati to find out the re-feed time. He told me, and then I had to ask, "Is that eastern time?" He went off on me, telling me he couldn't believe I didn't know the time zone for Cincinnati. I responded, "Sorry man, I'm out here in the Mountain Time zone and I wasn't sure." He paused for a moment and then asked, "There's a mountain time zone?"

The Best Halloween Story—EVER!

Note: this is a retelling of one of my favorite stories. In other words, I didn't make this up; I just put it into my own words.

It had been three days since my wife and kids had left to visit her parents. At first, I was looking forward to the peace and quiet. We had three daughters, all under the age of four, so finding any moments where there wasn't one crying, screaming, or banging on something was rare.

The first couple of nights were great. I came home with fast food, turned on some music, and sang at the top of my lungs without fear of waking up whatever child was asleep at the moment.

The third night, however, was something completely different. It was late October in New England. There were a few leaves that still clung onto the trees for dear life, but most had given in to peer pressure and had fallen to the ground.

I was sitting in our living room, watching TV and relaxing after a long day at work. A storm rumbled in during the course of the day and had covered the sky. Although it wasn't raining, the wind was blowing steadily, and the heavens were lit now and again with streaks of lightning followed by growling thunder.

My show was about to end when the power went out. I hated when that happened. No power meant no TV, no computer, no internet … nothing. I remembered thinking, What had people possibly done at night before electricity? I sat there for a moment debating my next move. I decided to light a candle and read—even though flickering light gave me headaches.

I tried to remember where my wife kept the candles and matches when there was a thump on the front porch. I nearly jumped out of my seat.

It sounded like something heavy landed on the porch. I thought it was probably a branch that had broken off in the storm and had fallen. I chided myself for being so jumpy. I was about to get out of my chair to investigate when there was a loud bang against the front door.

I froze in place, the hair on the back of my neck bristling. That couldn't have been a branch. Someone, or something, had hit the door. I sat there, my hands gripping the armrests of the chair, and listened.

There were no other sounds aside from the howling wind. And to think, I had been looking forward to the quiet.

Nothing happened for several moments aside from the occasional flashes of lightning. It took me a moment to realize that even though I was seeing the lightning, the thunder had stopped, though the storm had increased in its fury.

Finally, I gathered my courage. I decided I was not going to let things that went bump in the night get the best of me. I took a deep breath and stood up.

At that very moment, the front door burst open with such force that it ripped off its hinges. In the doorway, silhouetted by the lightning, was a coffin. It was deep black in color—so dark, in fact, it seemed to swallow the light around it.

I tried to will my feet to move, but they wouldn't. I tried to look away, but my eyes stayed locked on the coffin. I tried to scream, but the sound wouldn't come.

Slowly, the coffin tilted up, as if someone was standing it on its edge, though there was no one in sight. I couldn't move. It continued to raise itself up until it stood up completely.

Thunder sounded so loud and powerful that it shook the very house. It was as if all the thunder for the last few minutes had been stored up and released at once. At the same moment, the coffin lid swung open, revealing that it was empty inside.

For the briefest of moments, I was relieved. Part of my fear came from what was in the coffin. That relief soon vanished as the coffin slowly, purposefully, moved toward me.

Whether it was the coffin moving, or the thunder sounding, I'm not sure, but suddenly the flight part of my instincts kicked in. I ran to the closest room in the house—our bathroom. I locked the door and backed up into the tub, the only window to the room at my back.

I could hear the coffin scraping along the floor as it continued to approach. I realized that coming to the bathroom was not my smartest move. The window was too small for me to fit through. There was nowhere I could go.

My mind raced. What could I do? What was the old saying? Fight or flight. I had tried fleeing and that hadn't worked. I was left with the only other option. I looked around the bathroom, catching glimpses of objects here and there when the lightning briefly lit the area. I needed something heavy to use.

There! On the countertop was a large bottle of Robitussin. I took one step out of the bathtub and grabbed it, just as there was a loud bang at the bathroom door, though it stayed closed.

I retreated back to the tub, wielding my new weapon as if it was Excalibur.

Again, the lightning came, but no thunder. I stared at the door. I could feel my heart pounding in my chest.

Nothing happened for a long, drawn-out moment. I thought, *Maybe it went away. Maybe it could sense I was going to defend myself.*

The bathroom door crashed open and there was the coffin, the lid still open. It seemed to pause for a moment, and then again it started to move toward me.

With all my strength, I threw the bottle of Robitussin.

The coffin stopped.

Debating Rebating

It was time. I had had my cell phone for two years and I was eligible for an upgrade. With the advances in technology, my current phone was woefully out of date, and I was looking forward to getting something new.

After reviewing the options, I picked the phone I wanted. The store had all sorts of specials and such at the time. With my loyalty discount, their in-store promotions, and a manufacture rebate, I would be getting the phone for free—along with a free protective case. Granted, all the cases they had in stock were pink... (I was able to trade the pink one for a black one later.)

But then there was the matter of the rebate. As with most rebates, the process was fairly involved and if you didn't do it right, you were out of luck. To make matters more complicated, there was a twist to the process.

In order to get the rebate, not only did I have to fill out a lengthy form, but I had to include the customer agreement, a copy of the receipt, AND the barcodes off the side of the box the phone came in. For the barcodes, I had to physically cut the box and remove the side where the barcodes were located—this was made quite clear in the rebate instructions.

However, when I started to perform surgery on the box, I noticed that if I had to return the phone within the allotted time, I had to do so in an undamaged box or there would be a restocking fee. So I was stuck. If I sent in the barcodes (copies wouldn't work—they were clear on that), I would have to damage the box. But if the phone stopped working within a small time frame, I could return it, but only in a complete box. The company's solution was to give me six weeks to submit the rebate— longer than the time I had available to return the phone to the store in the perfect box.

But this causes yet another issue. Life is busy. There are always things demanding your time and attention. For me, if I don't take care of something right away, chances are it may be forgotten.

And that brings out the cynic in me. I have no doubt that companies offer rebates and make them fairly complicated to make it difficult for people to follow through. It's all well and good to say, "The phone is FREE ... after the rebate." But I'm sure they have their research that shows what percentage of people actually follow through on the rebate, and they adjust accordingly.

For example: if only 40% of the people actually follow through with the rebate, then the company can keep the other 60% of the rebate money. If they use that to their advantage, they could offer higher rebates to entice people to buy, knowing full well they won't have to pay out all the rebate money. Taking our example one step further, let's say the company could afford to do a $25.00 rebate, but instead, they offer a $50.00 rebate. Using the 40% / 60% assumption above, the company would be paying out less than half the claims, therefore paying less than the $25.00 they could afford. Yet the sales would be higher because $50.00 is a higher draw.

Again, I know it is cynical to think this way—but working in and with big corporations has given me plenty of reasons to be that way.

Here's a wild concept: stop with the games and actually charge a fair price without all the gimmicks to make it look like a better deal than it is.

Customer Service Ratings—To the Extreme!

I've noticed as a consumer that there has been a bigger focus on customer service surveys recently. I guess it makes sense. In an economy where jobs are hard to get and money is tight, businesses are doing whatever they can to make sure they retain their customers.

I'm all for receiving excellent service. If I go somewhere, I want to be treated nicely, not talked down to and certainly not treated like I'm a nuisance.

However, just like many things happening in corporate America, things can be taken too far. Think about the last time you went to your bank. Now, if I were to ask you the following questions, how would you rate your experience on a scale from 1 to 6 (6 being the best):

1. They went out of their way to please
2. They did things right the first time
3. They treated you like a valued customer
4. They made your business their top priority
5. They followed up and kept their promises

All right, have you figured out what you would have rated them? Did you give a perfect "6" in all the categories?

Did you know that if you scored anything less than a "6" in any of those categories, the person you "graded" would have a black mark given to them?

Let's take it to the next step. In any given month, 14,000 people go to a certain bank location. Of those 14,000, 10 people are randomly called. Of those ten, the minimum goal is for 80%, or 8 out of 10, to grade their visit with *all* perfect 6's across the board.

Any math whizzes out there that can figure the margin of error with those numbers?

I, sadly, have worked in such an environment. In my opinion, it is completely unfair—especially when the employee is held accountable for the non-perfect shop, even if they did all they could to take care of the customer.

Need more proof? Here is a true story that happened to me:

I was at a training class for a couple of days. When I returned to the bank that I managed, I was told that a customer had come in while I was gone. He was very upset because another location, a good hour away, had messed up his accounts and cost him fees. My team fixed the issue, refunded the fees, and escalated the issue to the area manager—because the man was *that* upset. I was contacted by the area manager and asked to buy a gift card for the customer to "make it up to him." I was also told at the time that I needed to update the man's zip code in the system.

So I did as I was asked. I even called the customer and left a voice message apologizing for what he had gone through and told him the gift card was on the way.

When our next surveys came in, this customer had been called and scored us very low. What was worse? The survey pinned me as the person who got the bad survey. How could that have happened? I had never even seen or spoken to the man—I had only left a message. The survey was triggered when I updated the man's zip code in the system.

The result? Not only did I lose a big chunk of my bonus for that month, but I was also written up for the low survey.

Why? Because it was policy that any time that low of a survey was received, the person had to be written up.

Black and White (and Angry All Over)

I once worked at a bank that prided itself on service. One day, a man came in to have his PIN reset on his debit card. I asked to see some ID to make sure I was changing the PIN for the owner of the card, and not someone who had found it. He told me he didn't have any ID and that he was in a hurry. Both of those statements were warning signs. I explained my reason for asking for ID. His response was to smack my arm and say, "You're a jerk!"

As he was leaving the bank, I said to him, "Sir, you just hit me, and that's not okay." He didn't say anything, but instead just left the bank. I remembered his name from seeing it on the debit card. I searched through the database and found a match. After that, I called my district manager (I was the manager at this branch) and told him a customer had hit me. Naturally, his response was, "What did you do to upset him?"

Fast forward a little bit. The incident was reported the proper way and the customer was contacted by my district manager. The man said he was mad because if he had been a white man, I would have never asked for ID. He said I was a racist. When I heard this, I was stunned. It took me a moment to think back and realize the man was an African-American.

Understand that I hold no ill will toward anyone based on their skin color or nationality. In the end, based on the eyewitness accounts of my fellow employees, the man's accounts were closed by the bank.

There were several things about the situation that were disturbing, but for me, the most disturbing was being accused of being a racist.

I hadn't thought about this event until a story came out of a church in Alabama that held a "Whites-Only Christian Conference." I read the article and then a number of the comments. The general tone was outrage. The pastor was called all sorts of names, racist being one of them. And then there was a comment that gave me reason to pause. The conference was held just a few days after the BET (Black Entertainment Television) awards. I read an article on that, and there were comments from readers that *it* was racist.

I guess what I can't wrap my head around is why so many people are quick to point to something that excludes them and then make a big stink about it. I can't imagine someone who attended the BET awards wanting to attend the Whites-Only Christian Conference and vice-versa.

Granted, some of the messages in these types of events are derogatory toward another group of people. That's terrible and it shouldn't happen.

I just have to shake my head and hope that one day people will stop seeing things in black and white. There's a whole range of colors out there to enjoy.

Epitaphs and Etiquette

Each year, the young women and young men (ages 12 to 18) in our church congregation have an "etiquette dinner." They learn about proper ways to behave on a date.

This year's dinner was close to Halloween, so my wife asked me to come up with some epitaphs for those who didn't follow the rules.

These will mean more if you are a member of The Church of Jesus Christ of Latter-day Saints, but even if you aren't, keep in mind that some of these guidelines may seem old fashioned today. For example, waiting until 16 to date, when slow dancing, making sure there is space between the couples and such.

Without further ado, here are some of the epitaphs:

The life of Riley
Is now at an end
Asking the question,
"Can't we just be friends?"

Rest now in peace
Our noble Aaron
Asked out Haley
In front of Darrin

Dear McKay was quite wise
He was never home late
But foolish in taking
Two girls on the same date

Please rest in peace
Our sweetest Kelley
She choked on butterflies
From inside her belly

No longer on this Earth
Is the unwise young Tom
When he told Carla
You remind me of Mom

Deep in this grave
Is our dear Nate
He tried to kiss
His very first date

At the zoo died Dallin
Dating a girl that he dug
Took too literally
Request for a bear hug

Dear Julia is gone
Not high, low, or in-between
'Cause she went on a date
Before she was sixteen

Madsen is quite dead
It's hard to believe
From trying to wipe
His mouth on his sleeve

Here lies the very young Alex
He felt like such a dork
Died from embarrassment
From using the wrong fork

The far too young Amy
Buried there in the sands
On a date with Derrick
Tried to drive and hold hands

Passed away is Daniel
On a date was this dude
Ate with his mouth open
Misunderstood "sea food"

Gone away is Brycen
Accidentally mistook
While picking up his date
Beautiful Blair for Brook

David didn't have much
Between his two ears
Asking twenty-six girls
To wait for two years

Not a Typical Tuesday Morning

Once a week I'd go into work early to spend time with my morning crew at the TV station. It was usually a Tuesday because it tended to be one of the less busy days. Before I left, I told my wife when I got home in the afternoon, we'd winterize our above ground pool. It was below a large tree, and if we didn't cover it early in the autumn, we'd have a pool full of leaves.

The morning newscasts went well. One of my directors wanted to talk with me about some issue or another, so after the studio was cleaned up, he and I sat down. It wasn't long before we got a knock on the door. "We just heard from the newsroom that a small plane hit one of the twin towers. They want us back on the air."

While this was not a normal occurrence, it didn't seem like a major news event. We gathered the crew back to the studio and control room. One of the morning anchors sat down at the news desk, and within moments we rolled the "breaking news" animation.

By this time, we had video feeds tuned in and were recording from several different sources. What we didn't have were details of what had happened. "That's a lot of smoke from a little plane," someone said as we watched the playback of the video.

The producer was sitting behind the director while the anchor adlibbed about what we did know—which wasn't much. Information starting filtering from the newsroom and was passed by the producer along to the anchor. There was a growing feeling of uneasiness, yet we were professionals and were staying on task. We were playing back some of the better video we had captured, and the anchor continued to comment on what we were seeing.

Then one of the production crew who was watching one of the other feeds said, "Oh <bleep!> Another airplane just hit the other tower! And it was a BIG plane!"

To this day, I can still picture this event in my mind. For a moment, no one said anything. It was like everyone was taking in a collective breath.

And then…chaos.

People started screaming to find video of what had just happened and cue it up to playback. The anchor stumbled over her words as the producer started yelling into her earpiece that another plane had crashed into the other tower. Over the intercom from the newsroom came several voices at once—each of them shouting and giving orders on what to do.

The director did her best to listen to all the commands thrown her way, several of them contradicting each other. Soon, we had the video cued up and we played it on the air. For the first time, we as a collective group watched the second tower get struck. For me, it felt like someone had hit me hard in the stomach.

The next several hours were a blur. I recall one of my audio technicians sitting in a corner and crying. I remember one of my camera operators getting so mad at whoever had done this that we needed him to take a walk to clear his head. Reports of other planes crashing came in. At the Pentagon. In a field in Pennsylvania. We had no idea what would happen next.

I tried to call home, but all the lines were busy. We stayed live on the air all day. As the Operations Manager, I made sure my people were fed and rotated through. We called the evening crew to come in early.

It seemed that every minute I was being pulled in many different directions. Sometimes as liaison between the newsroom and the production team, sometimes as decision maker, and over time, I became more of a comforter and supporter of my team as we all tried to make sense of what was happening before us.

In the late afternoon, we got a story from one of our reporters. A man had walked onto one of the overpasses that spanned I-95. In his hands was an American flag. He was waving it back and forth. When the reporter asked the man why he was doing this, his answer was along the lines of, "I had to do something. I just couldn't sit still. It may not seem like much, but I'm doing something."

Watching that story, I felt something I'd not felt since the events started that morning.

Hope.

$-9v + 4{:}40 \ am = @\char94\#\$\&\ !$

A classic lyric from the rock group Rush states, "Those who know what's best for us, must rise and save us from ourselves." Of course, in the context of the song, the composer is being satirical. However, in life it's astonishing how often we are constantly being saved from ourselves.

I'm still amazed at the story of the person who sued a certain restaurant because she spilled coffee on her and it was hot. Her complaint was that no one warned her the coffee was hot. So why are there not warning signs on ice cream cones warning us they are cold?

Please don't misunderstand—I am strongly in favor of anything that will keep me and my family safe. There are times, however, when these safety features or warnings get out of hand.

One night, our ten year old came to our room at 4:40 am complaining that her radio/alarm clock was making a beeping sound and was keeping her awake. My wife, bless her, came to her wits first and instructed her to unplug the radio/alarm clock. The ten year old said she already had, (smart girl!) but it was still beeping.

By now, I heard the beeping and recognized it as the smoke detector warning that the battery was getting low.

We've had our issues with smoke detectors before. In one of our previous houses, we had a smoke detector right by an inside door—and if you closed the door too quickly, the rushing air caused by the closing of the door would set off the alarm.

We've also had smoke detectors so close to the kitchen that when my wife was cooking certain items, (don't ask me what—she's the chef) the smoke detector would go off. I would joke that there had to be a better system to let me know dinner was almost ready.

To deal with the beeping that had woken my daughter, my wife and I got up and I verified that the sound was coming from the smoke detector in her room. No problem, right? Just replace the battery. What? It took a 9 volt? Who used 9 volt batteries for anything anymore? Hadn't those gone out of style the same time as VHS machines? We didn't have any of those on hand. All right, well, we'd just take the battery out and get one in the morning. There were smoke detectors in the hall, in the other girls' room, and in our main bedroom—we'd be fine.

I took the battery out of the smoke detector and that was the end of it, right? WRONG! The other smoke detectors in the house started that beeping now. To be clear: this was not the beeping that there was a fire, but a little "chirp" that happened every minute or so. Upon further inspection, I noted that the 9 volt battery was actually a backup in case the power failed, and each of the smoke detectors was wired into the house power—and linked together by some sort of communication network.

Because we had taken out the battery of one, the rest of the detectors then started freaking out. Of course, this had to happen at 4:40 in the morning—it couldn't happen while we were all awake.

We tried everything. I looked for a breaker to turn off the detectors—no luck. (Plus, it wasn't the safest thing to do, either.) Finally, I got out my tools and was going to just disconnect the darn thing. As I got up on a chair with tools in hand, I noticed there was a way to simply unplug the smoke detector from the house power. That did the trick.

So, the lesson learned here: always keep some extra 9 volt batteries on hand, or replace them every 6 months like you should. And while you are buying some extra 9 volts, you may want to pick up a few extra VHS tapes as well—you never know.

Spamettios

I have my little corner of the world. It's my man cave. It's where I do my writing, go to relax, and also to escape from the world. I'm a fairly organized person, though you may not think so by looking at my desk. It's got "a place for everything and everything all over the place" vibe to it. I know exactly where the bills are that need to be paid. The remote to my stereo system is within reach. My CDs (yes, I'm still fighting the good fight by buying CDs!) are on shelves to my right. In fact, everyone in my family knows that you don't mess with Daddy's man cave space.

For full disclosure, my man cave is really just one corner of a room my wife and I sectioned off from the rest of our house to be our office. (Our main floor had an open plan, so we walled off one section and put a door in the other entry to make the office.) The rest of this room I share with my wife. And when I say "share," I mean she has shelves of crafting supplies and all sorts of other things that moms need to keep a house running.

Just as my man cave is my "do not touch" area, the same can be largely said about the kitchen. Let me state up front, my wife is an excellent chef. She really enjoys cooking, which is one reason our marriage is so successful because I enjoy eating. My cooking skills, on the other hand, have much, if not *everything*, to be desired. In fact, while going to college, my motto was, "If it's not from a can, it's not for this man."

My wife isn't nearly as territorial of the kitchen as I am with my man cave space. She has a place where things are kept and such. I get that. But once in a while, I'll need to pinch hit if she's not feeling well or busy with meetings and so on.

There was one day when she was under the weather. She was resting on the couch. I volunteered to make dinner, and she said ok—which was a sign she wasn't in her right mind.

I went to the pantry to see what I could make. There were a couple of cans of spaghettios—the kids liked eating those. But in the back of my mind, I heard my wife's voice telling me we needed to have a balanced meal. I needed some sort of meat. No problem—there was a can of Spam.

So…I cut up the Spam and fried up little chunks of it while I was letting the spaghettios warm up. In the meantime, I cut up an apple into about eight uneven slices and put them on a paper plate. Once the Spam was cooked, I mixed the chunks into the spaghettios. Tada! Spamettios was born!

The kids actually really liked it and ate it all up. Once my wife was awake and feeling better, I told her what I had made. I still remember the look of horror on her face. To date, I've not been allowed to make dinner since then.

Pet Peeves

I don't have a pet named Peeves, although that would be a really good name for a dog, now that I think about it. Keep in mind; this is from a man who named his terrier-poodle "Armageddon." (He was so little, he needed a big name.)

I do, however, have things that bother me, though I can't always explain why. When managing people, I taught the principle "you can't always choose how you will emotionally react to something, but you can choose how you will *act* on those emotions."

I did some research and found several common pet peeves. From those, I noted some that I share with other people.

These include:

People who don't use their turn signal.

Let me be up front about this: I don't trust turn signals. Just because someone has their turn signal on, doesn't mean they will actually be turning. However, when I'm at a stoplight in one of those lanes where you can turn or go straight, and the person doesn't turn their signal on until *after* the light turns green, it bothers me.

Being asked my telephone number/account number by a service representative after I already entered it using the keypad on my phone.

This annoys me nearly as much as almost every automated message beginning with "Please listen carefully because our menu options have changed."

Hand in hand with this pet peeve are the automated messages that act like you are talking to a real person. For example, when they say, "Please wait a moment while I look up your information" and then you hear the recording of someone typing on a keyboard.

The plastic packaging that requires a degree in engineering to open.

I can't count how many times I've cut my fingers on these types of packages.

Finding that the end of a TV program hasn't recorded because its starting time was pushed back due to sports coverage running long.

This has gotten better over the years with DVR technology, but dang, for a while, I would always allow extra time when recording things Saturday or Sunday evenings.

When someone leaves a voice message and they speak their phone number so fast there is no way you can get it from one listen.

Maybe it's just the dyslexic person in me, but I really struggle with this one.

Texting while driving.

For heaven's sake! You are in control of a large moving object. Why not just put a blindfold over your eyes while you're driving? It's almost as safe.

People who write about pet peeves.

Oh, wait…

Don't Inhale

"When I was in England, I experimented with marijuana a time or two, and I didn't like it. I didn't inhale and never tried it again." –Bill Clinton

It was Labor Day weekend, and I was the manager on duty. The grocery store was one of those "no frills" places where people bagged their own groceries and took them out to their car. The floor was cement and the shelves were made out of wooden two-by-fours. The products were often still in the boxes they were shipped in, just cut open with easy access for customers to get what they needed. By far, we had the best prices, but the warehouse feeling of the store was too lowbrow for some people.

We were just about to close up for the night when a very loud whistling sound came from the far back corner of the store. It was like nothing I'd heard before. I tried to call the store manager, but he was out of town. The same was true for the store owner.

My assistant for the night was a cute girl who was half my size. We looked at each other in concern, and then decided to check it out.

As we got closer to the back corner, the sound was so loud we couldn't hear each other speak. The noise was originating from a large closet of sorts. There was a fine, white mist coming from the room, but it wasn't smoke—nothing smelled like it was burning.

I told my assistant to wait outside the closet and I would go check it out. (That was me being the brave macho manager dude.) I opened the door to find the room was filled with white mist. In the room were all sorts of machines—none of which I recognized. I stepped in further, trying to see what was causing the issue. Very quickly, I started to feel lightheaded, and there were spots dancing before my eyes. A still small voice in my head told me to get the heck out of there.

I turned, and panicked for a moment when I couldn't see the door. I was getting dizzy now and stumbled my way toward where I thought the door was. I found it and got out. The world was spinning now, and my assistant looked at me with fear showing in her eyes.

Somehow she helped me get to the front of the store—to this day, I'm not sure how. She must have been working out to get such a tall guy like me to move when my body didn't want to.

At the front of the store were the fire department and an ambulance. Even in my foggy state, I wondered who had called them. I found out later that the fire alarm had tripped.

The next part was fuzzy, but I recall being placed in the ambulance next to my assistant where we were both given oxygen. It turned out that one of the freezer compressors had sprung a leak and was spewing Freon into the air. Now, I don't know a lot about such things, but I was told breathing in Freon was bad—like too much and it could kill you kind of bad.

I survived, and I took a deeper lesson from it. Many times in my life, I've been placed in situations, both professionally and socially, where there are things around me that are dangerous. I'm not only talking about physical things, but also behaviors. At one of my places of employment where I ended up leaving on my own, the "air" was becoming polluted with negativity, micromanaging, double standards, and questionable ethical behaviors.

Just like when I was in the room with the white mist that was seemingly harmless at first, longer exposure would most certainly have led to unpleasant results. So, again, I listened to that still small voice in my head that told me to "Get out!"— and I did.

It's a Kind of Magic

There is a great series called *The Work and the Glory* which describes the trials pioneers went through while moving to the west—things that are hard for us to imagine. But as hard as it is for us to understand what it would be like to pull a handcart across Wyoming, I would imagine it would be just as hard for them to understand some of the things we take for granted every day.

If I went up to one of these pioneers, pulled out a small black box that fit in my hand, and told them I was going to talk to someone in China, they would think I was crazy. And what if I showed them I could do it? Could it be perceived as magic?

Or imagine going to King Arthur and using a laptop, showing him a satellite image of Camelot. Of course, it would have to be magic, wouldn't it?

I recall my 9th grade electronics teacher posing this question: "What would life be like without the use of electricity? How different would your life be?" It blew our minds to list all the different ways it would impact us.

Then he asked a question that *really* blew our minds: "What hasn't been invented yet, or isn't widely used, that twenty-five years from now, people are going to wonder how we lived without it?" Now, this is dating myself some, but I graduated high school in 1987.

So what is this "thing" that is now in everyday use that we would have a hard time living without? It's a little thing called the "internet." Yes, believe it or not, it wasn't until I was in college that I had any exposure to the internet. Even then, it was America Online with my speedy 2.4 K bits-per-second modem (I think that was how fast it was—or slow, as the case may be). Back then, you would type in a webpage, then go make a sandwich, take a jog around the park, come back home and take a shower followed by a little nap, and by then the page would be loaded.

Things we can see but don't understand may seem like magic, and perhaps that could even be considered magic.

This point was driven home to me one day by my then 3-year-old daughter Amy. After work one day, she was so excited to see me because she had a magic trick she wanted to show me. The trick was in the bathroom, which made me a bit leery since she had recently been potty trained.

Her trick was this: she rolled off about three feet of toilet paper. She lifted up both lids of the toilet and put one end of the paper in the water, with the other end hanging outside the bowl. She then closed the lids and flushed the toilet. Very soon, the toilet paper outside the bowl moved up and into the toilet. Tada! Magic!

Too Much "Motion" in Motion Picture

I get teased now and again about being the only man living in a house full of women (meaning my wife and my four daughters). But I really don't mind. Granted, instead of the rough and tumble of boys, we deal with the screaming and emotions of little girls. Again, it's all part of being a parent.

However, there are times when even I need to go and do manly stuff. Most of the time, to feel manly, I'll go to a movie that is targeted for the male gender. You know, action/adventure stuff with things blowing up, and often there are aliens involved.

One such movie was *Battle: Los Angeles*. From what I gathered, it was about the Earth being attacked by aliens with a big battle happening in Los Angeles. With the special effects they can do now, I thought, why not? It might be fun.

With my training in TV production and my ever developing skills as a writer, I can, at times, be critical of the production work or storytelling.

One clichéd opening is where the story starts with action, only to be stopped a few moments later with ominous words on the screen saying something like, "24 hours earlier…" and *Battle: Los Angeles* started that way—boom! Right into the action.

This is done quite a bit, and so I'm not overly critical (though having a story start out with a dream sequence which has you believing it's real drives me nuts).

But within the first few minutes of the film, I noticed the approach the filmmakers were taking. Basically, every shot had movement—in a herky, jerky way. Close-ups of people talking had the camera panning and tilting randomly. I gather the effect was to convey chaos and uncertainty. While I feel that can be effective in action sequences, does it work for a whole movie? My opinion would be a resounding "NO!"

When people are sitting in an office talking, what's up with the herky, jerky movements? When there is a tender scene where someone is baring his soul, does it work? No!

All these movements had an undesired side effect for me. I tend to get motion sickness fairly easily (something I passed on to my second daughter) and so trips on planes or to the amusement park require that I take motion sickness medications.

Maybe it's just me, but I don't think I should have to take motion sickness medication before going to a movie. *Battle: Los Angeles* was so bad in this regard that I ended up leaving during the final big action sequence for two reasons:

#1: I was getting sick to my stomach.

#2: I didn't really care what happened—the movie was that bad.

I'm sure I got some strange looks as I was leaving the theater during the final conflict, but I'm sure the looks I got when I was throwing up in a garbage can outside the theater from motion sickness were even stranger.

The Key to Flexibility

In an episode of *Star Trek: The Next Generation* the captain and chief medical officer are trapped on a planet and are trying to escape—only this story had a twist. For some reason—I don't recall why—they could now hear each other's thoughts. At one point, they come to a fork in the road, and the captain, being the captain, says, "It's this way."

The medical officer stops him and says, "Wait a minute! You don't really know that. You are just guessing." He ends up admitting that being a leader doesn't always mean you know all the answers—and sometimes you have to make your "best guess."

The key is to sound confident when you are doing it. Often, people need someone to believe in, or at least look to for guidance, even if that person is just guessing which is the best path to take.

In my non-writing life, I've held various management positions over the years. There are times I simply didn't know for sure the right answer, or the correct action to take. However, I've learned that sometimes you have to show confidence in your decision.

I'm not saying that there is anything wrong with showing weakness, or admitting you don't know. This is what I mean: there are times when people are following you and if they hesitate when you give the command, or haven't bought into what you are saying, it will fail, even if you made the right choice eventually.

Nowhere in my life has this been more evident than when I've directed live TV shows. You see, the thing about being "live" is, well, it's like life—it's unpredictable. I can't think of a program I directed where everything went according to plan. That's not to say it didn't turn out well, it just means that there were times when a decision came up that wasn't expected. As the director, your job is to tell everyone what to do and when. If you hum and haw, it's going to be too late. If you don't give the directions with confidence, the people taking your directions may have doubt and then hesitate. Like I noted before, sometimes that hesitation can cause even the right decision to fail.

At times, this would cause conflicts between the director and the producer. Let me explain. In live TV, the producer is like the architect, and the director is like the builder. The director looks at the blueprints the producer "drew" and then starts building. But again, with things happening live, the producers were always changing things on the fly. Sometimes they were minor tweaks like, "the carpet will be blue and not red" or "wallpaper instead of paint." Then there were other times when it was more along the lines of "Okay, move the bathroom that was on the third floor to the first floor and add a pool in the living room."

When the changes were too dramatic and given too late for me to make, I'd tell them "No." Producers don't like to be told no. In fact, that was one thing that my news director criticized me about. He said I wasn't being flexible enough. My response was always that we did whatever we could to accommodate the producers, but sometimes they would decide too late, or hum and haw, not wanting to make a decision. If they couldn't, or wouldn't, make the decision, often the director would have to make their best guess and sound confident about it or bad stuff would happen on air.

When I was preparing to leave that TV station to pursue other things, I was cleaning out my desk one day. I found a quote book I had been given by one of my employees about business life in general. I had to stop and laugh out loud when I came across a quote that fit the situation perfectly. It was: "The key to flexibility is indecision."

Yellow Car! I Win!

The western part of the United States of America is a big place. When you look on a map of the western USA, you'll see big states, most with straight lines for borders. Then you look to the east, you'll funky shaped states—many much smaller than those found out west. One of my daughters once pointed to Rhode Island and said, "Aw, how cute! A baby state!" (No offense intended to those wonderful folks in Rhode Island.)

My mother's parents (my grandparents) lived about four hours north of where I grew up in Utah. So how did my mom entertain four small children on such a long trip? And remember, this was before the invention of the DVD players. We'd play games!

One game we would play was the alphabet game. Basically, someone would say "go!" and then the game was on. The object was to find signs or words on cars that contained the letter of the alphabet you were on. You had to say the name of the letter, point to it if you could (not a good idea if you are the driver) and then say the word it was in. For example: "C, (point to the sign) Salt Lake City!"

Once someone used a word, no one else could use it. As you can imagine, we would get stuck on J, Q and Z. You would think X would be tough, but with all the exit signs, it was one of the easier ones. I still remember a building that advertised "Zims"—a store in SLC. I knew if I could get to the letter Z before we got to that building, I'd win the game.

When I traveled from Utah to Buffalo, New York for my internship, I drove alone. That was a long trip. I played the alphabet game a couple of times (I won every time), and then decided to make it harder. I played the number game. The goal was to go from 1 to 100—and to make it more of a challenge, the numbers had to be by themselves; they couldn't be part of a larger number. Two days and who knows how many miles later, I finished the game. I even pulled off the side of the road and did a little dance (driving alone for that long when you are not used to it can make you do odd things).

While taking a trip to Atlanta with just my wife, during the six-hour drive we got a little silly. There were these billboards that said in big letters: "Donate your boat!" So every time we saw a boat being pulled, or parked on the side of a street, we'd point to it and yell, "Donate your boat!"—sometimes with a Scottish accent. (Things happen like that when you are being silly.)

In Connecticut, I would drive my kids to school. If for no other reason, I did it to spend some time with them during those forever days. To keep them from bothering each other, we would play all sorts of different games. One was the fire hydrant game. Simple rules, really: count all the fire hydrants you can—everyone helps look for them as a group, seeing how many we could find.

Our latest game? If you see a yellow car, you point to it and say, "Yellow car! I win!" I'm not sure exactly what you win—perhaps some parting gifts like Rice-a-roni (the San Francisco treat) and a home version of the game. Granted, there aren't a lot of yellow cars inside my house.

Cute + Stupid = Cupid

"Oh, you think you're being charming!" is something I often hear from my wife. I tend to walk a fine line between being loving and silly—usually tripping and falling on the silly side.

A quote you'll hear from me time and again is, "I love the fact that even though we've been married over 20 years, I can still make you laugh." And it's true. My wife has heard all my jokes dozens of times over, so I'm forced to be spontaneously silly—and she finds it funny.

Early in our marriage, this would sometimes consist of throwing a cup full of cold water on her while she was taking a shower. (She'd do the same to me.)

Then there were times when we'd sit down to eat dinner and she'd get up to get something from the kitchen. I'd take her utensils and hide them. She'd come back, we'd say the blessing on the food, and as we were about to eat, she would get a perplexed look on her face. The whole time, I would act as if nothing had happened.

One of my favorite silly things to do was to "stack the cards" when we'd play one of our favorite card games. While I was "shuffling," (I was actually just having the cards make shuffling sounds) I'd put the cards in an order where she'd have an amazing hand. However, mine would be just a wee bit better.

This trick would only work when she was getting us some snacks to munch on while we played, as well as because she rarely cuts the deck.

On more than one occasion, her pillow would somehow disappear while she was getting ready for bed, and I was already in bed reading. Spooky!

But this isn't a one way street. Oh no. She can be just as silly.

One night, I had gotten a drink and a bowl of chips. I placed them on our kitchen island with the intention of taking them to my computer to enjoy while I wrote. But before I left the kitchen area, I used the bathroom to powder my nose. When I returned, the cup and bowl were both there—just with nothing inside them. She was doing the dishes and acted like nothing had happened.

All this brings me to one of my wife's favorite quotes: "Anyone can be passionate, but it takes true lovers to be silly."

All of the Above

In my 8th grade gym class, we learned the rules of basketball. We were even given a test. Now, you may ask, how do you take a written test in gym class? The answer? We would lie on our bellies with pencils provided by the teacher and use the floor as a desk top. I'm sure it looked odd to anyone passing by.

One of the questions was, "What are the two major defenses?" A less than bright (but large and strong) classmates answered, "Nuclear and Atomic."

To be fair, it was the early 80s and in the middle of the Cold War, so the threat of nuclear war was on everyone's mind. However, it did introduce me to the concept of learning how to be a good test taker.

Often in college, I spent more time figuring out what the teacher wanted, and less time trying to understand the material. I could memorize facts and such, but applying that knowledge was a different matter.

One of my required classes for my Communications / Broadcasting Degree was learning about public relations. My teacher was a professional PR person and missed many of the classes she should have taught. In her place, she had her teaching assistant (TA) pinch hit. In preparing for our first test of the semester, the TA had an after class study session. I took advantage of it because I could really care less about PR—I was learning to become a TV director, so my heart wasn't in the subject matter, but I still wanted a good grade.

The TA went over each question and told us the things to study to answer the questions correctly. This was a level 400 class for seniors, so it was pretty intense. Before the test, I studied and reviewed, and studied and reviewed some more. I went into the test feeling pretty confident.

The next class, our main teacher stormed into the room and slammed her books on the table. Her opening line was, "Do you all think this class is a joke?"

With wide eyes, we all looked at each other, wondering what she was talking about. "You all failed the test! Didn't any of you take this seriously?" We couldn't help but notice our TA wasn't there that day.

One of my classmates spoke up, "I don't understand. How could we *all* fail it?" She huffed back, "Well, that is what we are going to find out."

She then proceeded to hand back our tests. My guess was that she must have worn out several red pens in grading them. As we started going over the test, the teacher would read the question, and then explain the answer. The odd thing was that the answers didn't resemble what the TA had taught us.

After half a dozen or so questions, with various people pointing out that this wasn't what the

TA had taught us, she finally demanded, "Well, who are you going to believe? Me or the TA?"

It was my turn to speak up for the class. My response? "Honestly, I didn't think we had to choose—or was that part of the test?"

Fun With Palindromes

A palindrome is a word or group of words that reads the same forward as it does backwards. Example: "I did, did I?" (Granted, that is a fairly lame one.)

For giggles, here is a short story full of palindromes. Can you find them all? The answers follow the story and are in **bold**.

Hannah looked at Bob with a level gaze. Her face was getting redder by the minute. "Desserts, I stressed!"

"Wow, calm down! I did get your note, as well as the other eight you sent. It wasn't clear. I had Otto and Dennis look at them as well. Some men interpret nine memos different ways."

Hannah frowned. "And whose radar didn't pick up on the desserts?"

"It wasn't me or Otto. I believe Dennis sinned on this one."

"Dennis? That man is drab as a fool, aloof as a bard," Hannah said. "This civic event is going to be the end of me. Nothing is right. Did we at least get the right main course? These are members of the salami board, after all."

Bob mumbled under his breath, "Go hang a salami; I'm a lasagna hog."

"What was that?" Hannah asked.

"Nothing."

Hannah stomped around the meeting hall. "And what about all these cats? They have to be moved! Stack cats five high if needed. I don't want us to step on no pets. Bah! These cats are crazy!"

"They aren't crazy. They are just old—senile felines. I'll move them."

"You shouldn't let Ma keep so many cats," Hannah complained.

Bob turned and faced Hannah. "She has a kind heart. So do I. Ma is as selfless as I am."

"Too soft-hearted." Hannah nodded.

"Don't nod," Bob said. "I hate when you do that. Don't lose focus. This is a big event. What is the salami board's motto? Oh, yes. 'Are we not drawn onward, we few, drawn onward to new era?' We should be honored they chose to have the event here."

Hannah walked to the decorative fireplace. "Did the salami arrive yet?"

"No trace; not one carton."

Stomping her foot, Hannah said, "Nothing is going right! Even this place is decorated all wrong. From the goldenrod-adorned log to the tin mug to the brown kayak."

At that moment, Anna and Nita walked in.

"Yo, banana boy!" Anna called.

Bob scowled. "Don't call me that. I don't like fruit. No banana, no lemon, no melon, nothing."

"Okay, how about I say 'Yo, Bob! Mug o' gumbo, boy!' instead?"

"Stop it, you two," Hannah said. "We need to clean this area up. Speaking of mugs, Anna, get this tin mug out of here."

Anna turned to her companion. "Hmm. What to do? A tin mug for a jar of gum, Nita?"

"Yes, gum will bombard a drab mob with happy feelings," Nita replied.

Hannah approached Anna. "Did you do as I told you to get rid of the wart on your hand? We can't have you serving the salami board with a warty hand. I can get more straw if you need it."

"Straw? No, too stupid a fad; I put soot on warts," Anna replied. "It will be gone in time."

Hannah gave Anna a stern look. "It better. We can't have you looking like an oozy rat in a sanitary zoo."

"I heard that Tarzan raised Desi Arnaz' rat," Bob chimed in. "True story!"

Hannah growled at Bob. "You aren't helping! If I had a boot, I'd kick you."

"Too bad I hid a boot." Bob smirked.

(The answers are next)

Hannah looked at **Bob** with a **level** gaze. Her face was getting **redder** by the minute. "**Desserts, I stressed!**"

"**Wow**, calm down! I **did** get your note, as well as the other eight you sent. It wasn't clear. I had **Otto** and Dennis look at them as well. **Some men interpret nine memos** different ways."

Hannah frowned. "And whose **radar** didn't pick up on the desserts?"

"It wasn't me or Otto. I believe **Dennis sinned** on this one."

"Dennis? That man is **drab as a fool, aloof as a bard**," **Hannah** said. "This **civic** event is going to be the end of me. Nothing is right. **Did** we at least get the right main course? These are members of the salami board, after all."

Bob mumbled under his breath, "**Go hang a salami; I'm a lasagna hog.**"

"What was that?" **Hannah** asked.

"Nothing."

Hannah stomped around the meeting hall. "And what about all these cats? They have to be moved! **Stack cats** five high if needed. I don't want us to **step on no pets**. Bah! These cats are crazy!"

"They aren't crazy. They are just old—**senile felines**. I'll move them."

"You shouldn't let Ma keep so many cats," **Hannah** complained.

Bob turned and faced **Hannah**. "She has a kind heart. So do I. **Ma is as selfless as I am**."

"Too soft-hearted," **Hannah** nodded.

"**Don't nod**," **Bob** said. "I hate when you do that. Don't lose focus. This is a big event. What is the salami board's motto? Oh, yes. '**Are we not drawn onward, we few, drawn onward to new era**?' We should be honored they chose to have the event here."

Hannah walked to the decorative fireplace. "Did the salami arrive yet?"

"**No trace; not one carton**."

Stomping her foot, **Hannah** said, "Nothing is going right! Even this place is decorated all wrong. From the **goldenrod-adorned log** to the tin mug to the brown **kayak**."

At that moment, **Anna** and Nita walked in.

"**Yo, banana boy!**" **Anna** called.

Bob scowled. "Don't call me that. I don't like fruit. No banana, **no lemon, no melon**, nothing."

"Okay, how about I say '**Yo, Bob! Mug o' gumbo, boy**!' instead?"

"Stop it, you two," **Hannah** said. "We need to clean this area up. Speaking of mugs, **Anna**, get this tin mug out of here."

Anna turned to her companion. "Hmm. What to do? **A tin mug for a jar of gum, Nita**?"

"Yes, gum will **bombard a drab mob** with happy feelings," Nita replied.

Hannah approached **Anna**. "**Did** you do as I told you to get rid of the wart on your hand? We can't have you serving the salami board with a warty hand. I can get more straw if you need it."

"**Straw? No, too stupid a fad; I put soot on warts**," **Anna** replied. "It will be gone in time."

Hannah gave **Anna** a stern look. "It better. We can't have you looking like an **oozy rat in a sanitary zoo**."

"I heard that **Tarzan raised Desi Arnaz' rat**," **Bob** chimed in. "True story!"

Hannah growled at **Bob**. "You aren't helping! If I had a boot, I'd kick you."

"**Too bad I hid a boot**." **Bob** smirked.

Failure *is* an Option

I'm going to go out on a limb to make a bold statement: humans aren't perfect. I know, I know, call me a radical. This statement may be as shocking as when people claimed the world was round, and not flat. Or that the Earth revolves around the sun and not vice-versa.

And since people aren't perfect, they make mistakes. I personally learn more from my mistakes than from my successes. To that end, let's just say I'm a wise man for that very reason.

Does that mean that since we know that we make mistakes that we shouldn't try to be successful? No, I'm not suggesting that at all.

In my professional life, I've managed hundreds of people (not all at the same time), and I've enjoyed watching many of them grow and learn. It's wonderful to see them master their craft over time. As they were learning, did they make mistakes? Heck, yeah. It was those who learned from these mistakes who ended up being successful.

Sadly, from my point of view, we are moving to a world where if you aren't "perfect," you aren't successful. I've heard it called the "Hero or Zero" philosophy. And it's a shame. No one can be the hero all the time.

At one of my jobs, the company was really coming down on the employees to hit some lofty goals—not just some, but all of them. Even if you were a "rock star" (their term) in 4 of the 5 areas, you were still considered a failure. They went as far as to adopt a new motto: "Failure is not an option."

Here's another wild concept: being imperfect isn't the same as being a failure. I think that is worth repeating: being imperfect isn't the same as being a failure.

Still need convincing? Have you noticed how "Fail" has become a popular term for something that didn't turn out right? And if it was really bad? It's an "Epic Fail."

This concept of "all or nothing" was driven home to me when one of my teams was audited by the company operations person. After spending two days going over all our records, it was time for her to review her findings. Overall, we did very well—aside from one document. On this particular document, several items needed to be recorded every day along with the initials and date. There were lines for several days, so you could have around 50 entries on a single paper.

On one of the entries, the person filling it out put the date in the wrong format. Instead of putting 12 March, they wrote 3/12.

The auditor said that because of that mistake, that whole document was a failure. I asked, "So you are telling me that because of one little mistake (that basically said the same thing), we're getting a failing grade on the whole document?"

The answer was, "Yes, it has to be perfect."

I was obviously upset by this close-minded thinking. We continued down the rest of the audit, where we had done very well. Then, toward the bottom, I noticed a typo in one of her sentences.

I turned the paper around on the desk and pointed to it. Her response was, "So what? It's a typo; you still know what it means."

My response? I grabbed a red pen, circled the typo, and then in big letters at the top wrote "FAIL."

I handed it to her and said, "Sorry, but it has to be perfect."

Weighing the Weight of Waiting

"In a world of what we want, is what we want, until it's ours" is a lyric from Train's song *Calling All Angels*. Pretty deep insight, right? After all, how many times have we desperately wanted something, and when we finally got it, we took it for granted?

Is that just how we are as human beings? Or is it something else? Another popular saying is "The best things in life are worth waiting for." Why is that exactly? Is it because once we actually get it, we say, "WOW! That was so worth the wait!" Let me suggest another meaning to that saying: it isn't the actual getting of the item that makes it "worth it." It's *because* we had to wait to get it.

All right, that's a deep concept—but hang in there with me for a moment. Let me give you an example. My oldest daughter, Kelley, really wanted an iPod Touch for her 14th birthday—so much so, she told my wife and me about it 6 months in advance. With her birthday not until September, and the high cost of an iPod Touch, my wife and I struck a deal with her: If she would save up $100, we would pay the rest for the iPod. That gave her 6 months to save.

As a 14-year-old, she couldn't exactly go out and get a job. She could, however, save her allowance as well as the money she would get from occasional babysitting gigs. I don't know about you, but the thought of saving $100 when I was 14 seemed downright impossible—but she did it.

A few weeks before her birthday, it was announced that there was a new version of the iPod Touch coming out. It was so new, we had to order it ahead of time to make sure we'd have it for her birthday.

It arrived, and she knew we had it, but we told her she needed to wait until her birthday—which was about a week away. She was so excited she actually counted down the days. Finally, the big day arrived and she was given her iPod Touch.

I have no doubt in my mind that had we gotten the iPod back in March when she first wanted it, it wouldn't have meant that much to her. Plus, she wouldn't have gotten the newer version. I am so proud of her for saving up the money and waiting for it. It was a valuable lesson—for her and for me.

I believe it wasn't actually getting the iPod Touch that made the whole experience wonderful; it was overcoming the challenge of saving the money and waiting for it that truly made it worth it.

Often what we want is only a mouse click away. Before clicking, perhaps we should pause for a moment and ask ourselves, "Is this worth waiting for?"

Honestly! It's an Orange!

Any type of art form will have its critics. Actually, that's a fairly negative way of phrasing that. Let me try again. Any type of art form will have its fans. And of these fans, many will have different reasons for liking something.

When reading reviews of *The Hidden Sun*, it became clear to me that men liked the action while women liked the romance. Almost across the board, people enjoyed the characters and the twists and turns. Many struggled with the names I invented, so much so that I added a whole new page on my website dedicated to how to pronounce them, which was later included in the second edition.

It reminds me of an art class I had to take in high school. In order to graduate, you had to fulfill certain requirements. Example: you needed to have a certain number of math or science or English classes and such. One of these requirements was art. It could be fulfilled if you were in the band (I don't play an instrument), or in chorus (I have a severe case of athlete's voice), or drama (I was rather shy back then) or art classes. I defaulted to the art class—since there was nothing else I could really do.

On the first day of class, the teacher set out a bowl of fruit and asked us to draw it. I looked at my classmates as began. Some had special drawing pads, and many had several different types of pencils—

various widths and such. Me? I pulled out a lined paper and my #2 pencil. I think I even sharpened it before I started to draw.

The teacher had us hand in our work at the end of class. When I turned mine in, she asked, "Is this some kind of joke?" I answered, "No. I did my best." Her response? "What are you even doing in this class?"

That was a good question. My response? I never went back to that class again. I would just skip it, or "sluff" it as we called it back then. Yes—I failed the class. Fortunately, I was able to get into the radio program we had at the school, which ended up counting as my art requirement (though I went in as an engineer to fix and maintain the equipment).

The lesson I learned from this? You can't please everyone when you are doing anything creative—whether it be art, music, or writing.

Final case in point: A good friend of mine took an art class in college. One of his first assignments was to draw a tree. With pencil and paper in hand, off he went on his quest. He found a particularly attractive tree and sketched it. The next class, the teacher had the students bring up their drawings and he would grade them from 1 to 10, 10 being the best. After a quick glance over my friend's drawing, he wrote the number "6" in red at the top. My friend was none too pleased.

The teacher said that they could do the assignment again if they wanted to improve their score. Off my friend went, this time adding more detail and shading to the tree. He spent a good couple of hours working on it. Again, he took it to the teacher, and again, the teacher gave it a quick glance over and wrote the number "6" on it.

My friend was given one last chance to improve his score. He set aside a whole Saturday and drew the tree. He caught little nuances in the bark he had missed before and added them. He played with how the light shone through the branches and leaves. He added some of the ground around the base of the tree to show the root system. It was amazing.

Excited, he took his drawing to the next class. The experience had helped him see things he had not seen before. Proudly, he displayed his work to the teacher. After a quick look over, the teacher took his red pen and on the paper wrote a big number "6."

Muscle Memory

I was sitting in an office with one of my fellow managers. We were about to get on a conference call. I was fairly new to the company, and she was helping me finish up the training. I asked her if she needed me to look up the number, and she said not to bother; she had it memorized. It wasn't the first time I'd offered to help with something just to be turned down because she acted like she knew it all and I was a distraction at best. When it came time to dial the number, she didn't even look at the phone while her fingers quickly danced on the keypad. A moment passed and then over the speakerphone came the following words (or something similar): "Hey, sexy! Looking for some hot one-on-one chat?" I looked at the other manager as she quickly disconnected the call. "This darn phone," she said. "It's old and the numbers are always getting stuck." When she redialed the number, I noticed that she did so more carefully, and this time she referenced something from her rolodex.

There are some numbers I call often and the only way I can remember them is to actually dial the number and watch as the muscle memory in my hand keys it in. The concept is pretty wild to me—that my body can be trained to do something and it will do it without me really having to think about it.

Like what? Well, driving, typing, walking and chewing gum at the same time…

I'm certainly no expert on this subject, but I would say that is why musicians practice so much—they are training the memories in their muscles to react a certain way when they want a certain outcome. The old saying of "practice makes perfect" definitely carries some weight.

My wife has carte blanche to decorate the house as she sees fit. The two areas I'm allowed to have a say in are my side of the bed and my desk in our home office. At least I have those. And I'll be the first to admit that the house looks very nice because of this agreement.

One thing in my office is a trophy I won several years ago. I'm tall at 6'3," and back in the day, I was fairly athletic. I never tried out for any of the sports teams in high school, but we had something that took its place. It was sort of like city league softball, except it was done within our church. I grew up in Utah, where there are a lot of Mormon congregations, or "wards" as they are called. The young men in our ward would be on a softball team. The church would set up a season schedule followed by a round of tournaments.

Back when I was a teenager, we played outside a lot. One of our favorite games to play was called "Indian Ball." I have no idea where the name came from, and I'm pretty sure it isn't politically correct, but there you have it. It was basically softball with only four players—two on each team. I won't go into the details, but playing it helped us practice all the skills of hitting, throwing and fielding. I was a pretty fast runner, so I liked to play the outfield.

We would play this game for hours upon end, often playing until it got too dark to see. But in doing so, I really developed some pretty decent skills. I learned how to switch hit (meaning hitting both left and right handed) as well as become a darn good outfielder, if I do say so myself.

The softball season before my senior year in high school, we had a really good team. We won the regular season and went on to win the next several rounds of tournaments. I'm not sure how many we won, but we ended up in the "area" championship game. If I were to hazard a guess, I'd say there were roughly 400 teams in this area, so it was a big deal getting there.

Before the championship game, our coach brought in a hitting instructor to help us tune up for the final game of the year. After watching me hit, he said, "You have more power from the right side—you are more of a slap hitter from the left. You should hit from the right side."

For the whole year, I had basically hit from the left side because I could cross up the defense and get on base a lot. I'd only really hit from the right side if we needed a deep fly ball to sacrifice a runner home. But the hitting instructor was pretty adamant that I hit from the right side.

How did things go for the last game? Well, my first at bat was a deep fly ball to left that was caught right in front of the fence. My second at bat had the same result. The game was uncharacteristically low scoring, so I only got one more at bat. I went to step into the left hand batter box but my coach yelled for me to hit from the right side. I went to the right side and tried to do more of a slap hit to get on base, but I grounded out to short instead. My muscle memory simply hadn't been trained for what I was trying to do that last game.

The good news is that we won—though I had my worst hitting game of the season.

I often wonder how I would have done that last game if I didn't try to be something others thought I should be.

The Tribe has Spoken

It's all about being the best. Isn't it? Case in point: how early are the stores opening on the day after Thanksgiving? Does it seem to be getting earlier every year? It seems that way to me. It's almost like, "Hey! Our competitor is opening at 6:00 am! We need to open at 5:30!" Then next year: "Hey! They opened at 5:30 am, we need to open at 5:00!" At this rate, stores will be opening up early on the day after Christmas for the following Christmas.

But it isn't just opening up early. One year, I was especially turned off by an ad from Best Buy where they had animated characters make a big deal about how the store and support folks would be working Christmas. Why? So they could outdo their competition. Never mind all those folks that would have to work instead of being home with their families.

That's why I applaud companies that stand up for what they believe in, no matter what the others are doing. Chick-Fil-A? Closed on Sundays. B&H photo and video store? Closed Friday at 2:00 pm and all day Saturday. Whether their beliefs are the same as mine doesn't matter. I'm just happy there are those in the world that see that there are certain lines you don't cross.

Time for a confession: my wife and I love to watch the TV show *Survivor*. Yes, yes, there are some of you out there that might condemn us for such an action, but let me explain why I enjoy it so much. The show is really a microcosm of the world around us. The goal is to be the last man (or woman) standing at the end of the game. I won't go into all the details, but there are certain rules that need to be explained to prove my point.

First, there are about 18 or so people that start the game. One by one they are voted off by the rest of the players (their "tribe"). Now the tricky part comes about halfway through the game. Why? Well, the people voted off go onto something called the "jury." This jury of people will pick the final winner. In other words, the final contestants will be held accountable for their actions.

The motto of the game is "Outwit, Outlast, Outplay." The show has been on for something like 20 seasons (2 seasons per year), and all sorts of people have won. There was a recent contestant who got to play in back to back seasons. He was mean. He was a bully. He did things to cause conflict with his teammates (like burning socks, draining their water supply, telling lies to anyone who would listen). He did it to gain control.

In both cases he weaseled his way to the end…and lost. Why? Because he eventually was judged for his actions. Had he made it near the top? Yes. In the end, did he win? No. And to read interviews about him later, he kept saying how the game was stupid and that he should have won.

As I remember it, in *Death of a Salesman*, the main character becomes a salesman because when he was young, he attended the funeral of a salesman and was amazed by how many people were there and how respected this man was. That's the kind of funeral he wanted. This young man ended up having a miserable life, and in the end, very few attended his funeral.

Why? He was doing something he didn't enjoy and it reflected in his life.

You Load 16 Tons, and What Do You Get?

Clear Creek, Utah was where I went to summer camp between my 5th and 6th grade years. We spent a week learning all sorts of things about nature and the wilderness and so on. Naturally there was the story of the "hermit" who haunted the area—it seems every camp has to have a ghost story attached to it, or it doesn't qualify as a summer camp.

One of the many things we learned there was about the old west. Back then, some of the more unscrupulous business men came up with a plan to keep men working for them. They would hire people to come work in the middle of nowhere to mine or do any number of other jobs. Because they were so far from anywhere, the workers couldn't pop over to Target to get their needs. So what did they do? Simple: the owner created a general store where the workers could buy supplies. And even better, they didn't have to pay for them. Instead, the owner would deduct the goods from the worker's pay. Sounds pretty good, right?

Unfortunately, some of these owners figured out that if they charged more for the goods than what the workers could make, then the workers ended up owing the company money—and would have to work to pay it off. It was a downward spiral for the workers.

I believe this inspired the song "16 Tons" by Tennessee Ernie Ford (who was actually from Tennessee, believe it or not). It was one of the songs we learned at summer camp. The chorus went:

You load sixteen tons, what do you get
Another day older and deeper in debt
Saint Peter don't you call me 'cause I can't go
I owe my soul to the company store.

It's hard to believe people could get away with something like that, but times were tough and people would do anything to get and keep a job. Hmmm. Not so unlike today.

There is an interesting word in the business world. It is "salary." If you make a salary, you don't qualify for overtime pay. What this equates to is owners and companies using that as an excuse to work someone as many hours as they can.

But those hours don't have to be at your physical job location. With the increase in technology, we can now access our work at home. Heck, you can even have access in your hand with a mobile internet device. There are also the company issued cell phones, so they can reach you "whenever it is important." It's amazing how many things are "important" these days.

The line between home life and work continues to become more blurred. And I am going to go out on a limb and say that isn't a good thing. If you are married, you need time to spend with your spouse to keep your relationship healthy. If you are a parent, you need time with your kids. And yes, you even need time for yourself. I honestly believe people work better when they have a good work / life balance.

If good old Tennessee Ernie Ford were to write that song today, it might go:

You sent sixteen emails, what do you get
Another day older and deeper in debt
Saint Peter don't you call me 'cause I can't go
I'm a salaried employee and my boss will say no.

Get Lost

There is a great song by Mike Oldfield called *To Be Free* off his *Tres Lunas* album. (Can you still call them albums? We can't really call them CDs or LPs or Cassettes or 8-Tracks...) One of the lines in the song is "And if I get lost, I really don't mind. I'm free—doin' just fine."

At one point in my book *The Hidden Sun*, one of the characters goes to a favorite garden of hers and hopes to get "lost" in it—to forget the troubles of the world for a while. It may sound strange that someone would intentionally get lost, but there is a certain freedom attached to it.

Once in a while, I'll take a different way home. Or perhaps I'll take a road I've bypassed before just to see where it takes me. There was even a game we played when we were teenagers. My car back then was a killer Datsun 200SX—yes, that was pre-Nissan. It was a sweet ride. I had a friend who told me it looked like a spaceship—all low to the ground with its hatchback fitted with sun blind things. It also had a digital clock that showed the seconds!

We would get into my car and drive until we came to a stop light or stop sign. If we stopped when the seconds were odd, we would turn left. If the seconds were even, we would go right. For zero? That meant to go straight.

This game led us to some pretty strange places. Keep in mind, this was in Utah Valley—a pretty darn safe place to live. There was one night it took us into Provo, up against the mountains. We found ourselves driving down a back alley behind some pretty big houses. Behind one of these houses was an old stone wall. In the stone, there were shapes of crosses—the kind you would see on a Crusader's shield or knight's crest. It was kinda freaky. This was about the same time the third Indiana Jones movie had come out, so we let our imaginations run wild and claimed we had found where they buried the Knights who were protecting the Holy Grail.

To this day, if I need to clear my head, or look for inspiration for the next section of whatever project I'm working on, I'll go try to get lost. Granted, more often than not, after I've found that peace or inspiration, I'll have to pull out my GPS to find my way home.

Twin Memories

One of the many places I've called home was the wonderful town of Twin Falls, Idaho. "Twin," as the locals call it, is one of those central towns surrounded primarily by farming communities. Probably its greatest claim to fame is the failed jump of Evel Knievel over the Snake River Canyon back in 1974. (Look it up on the web if you have no idea what I'm referring to.)

It was actually a great place to live, and like most areas of the world, there were some quirky things about it. First off, it was named after a set of falls from the Snake River. At a certain point of the river there was a big land section in the middle, with the river going around either side and then off a deep drop, causing "Twin Falls." Well, at least there were two falls until one was dammed up and they put in a power station or something. Perhaps they should have changed the name of the town to "Single Falls" or "The Town Previously Known as Twin Falls" with just a symbol representing two waterfalls as the official logo.

That part of the country is also next to the stunning Sawtooth Mountains. As a prominent landmark, it was the inspiration for many of the businesses and schools in the area. There was Sawtooth Elementary, Sawtooth Vacuum, Sawtooth Heating and Air Conditioning, and my personal favorite: Sawtooth Dental. Granted, that last one could be taken the wrong way.

Twin Falls had several car dealerships. Though sadly it seems they have since changed owners, while we were there, the local Ford dealership was owned by Jules Harrison. I still recall the sign out front. In small letters was the name "Jules" followed by large, bold words that read "Harrison Ford." (True story!)

Then there was the cruisin' of Blue Lakes Blvd on Friday night (or was it Saturday, or both?). Blue Lakes was the main street down the heart of the town. On cruisin' nights, people would drive up and down Blue Lakes with windows down, music blaring, girls trying to pick up guys, guys trying to pick up girls, and me, trying to get home after directing the 10 o'clock newscast. On more than one occasion, girls would drive up next to me and would honk and wave (methinks they were partaking of the strong drink). I found this particularly humorous because I was driving what my wife and I called our B.M.W. (Big Mormon Wagon—AKA Minivan.) It should have been obvious if I was cruisin' for chicks (as they called it) that I wouldn't drive something shouted, "I'm married and have a lot of kids!"

But I think my favorite memory of Twin Falls was also one of the more surreal experiences I've had in my life. I first started training at the TV station in the mornings. On my second day to work, I was a bit more familiar with the route, so I got to look around while driving. It was still dark, but store signs were lit up. One of these stores was called "Tuesday Morning." I'm not sure what type of store it was, but I remember thinking, "Wait, there is a store there named Tuesday Morning, and right now it is Tuesday morning. When I drive by here tomorrow, will it say Wednesday Morning?"

The answer? Go to Twin Falls and see for yourself.

The Name Game

Ever wondered how or why an author picks the names for their characters? I'm sure you'd have as many different answers to that question as there are authors.

I'll bet some authors pick names because they sound cool. One of the TV shows my wife and I really enjoy is *Castle*. Strangely enough, the show has nothing to do with medieval times. Rather, the main character's name is Rick Castle, played by one of my favorite actors, Nathan Fillion (from another one of my favorite shows, *Firefly*).

Rick Castle is an author of murder mysteries. He creates a character named Nikki Heat based on one of the NYC detectives he shadows on her job. Why Nikki Heat? Well, you'll have to admit that if you are imagining an attractive and smart NYC detective, Nikki Heat works better than, oh, let's say Bertha Flabbersnoogle.

Actually, I've often found that names seem to be picked based on how they sound. Some classic examples are in Dickens's *A Christmas Carol*. The name Scrooge sounds to me like an old curmudgeon. At the same time, would the name Tiny Tim have the same impact if he was named Tiny Bubba or Tiny Rocko?

When I pick names for my characters, I do something a little different. I actually research what the name means. For example, in *The Hidden Sun*, there is an owner of a candle store named Chandler. Do you know what the name Chandler means? Well, it means "candle seller." True story!

But it isn't enough to have the name mean something. It also has to look and /or sound like the character. That is the tricky part, but it also helps me create characters that are unique.

And then there are reasons people name their kids the way they do. Sometimes they are named after friends or family members. For example, my middle name, Lloyd, is from my maternal grandfather. My little brother? He was named after my paternal grandfather.

For our children, two of my four daughters' first names are directly from friends and family members, while the other two names, we just liked in and of themselves. In all cases, their middle names are directly from friends or family members.

Sometimes parents name their kids with all the same first letter. Like Quinton, Quinn, Qadir and Quetzalcoatl. (You have to be creative if you use the letter "Q.")

For my wife and me, we did it sort of backwards. Each of our girls' names end with an "e" sound, like Kimberly. And even then, not all their names end with a "y." Did we do that on purpose? Not at first. It just sort of worked out that way for the first three—Kelley, Emily and Amy. As for the fourth one? Stephanie. Yes, I will most certainly say that how her name ended played a big part in picking her name.

Just for giggles, what would you name a tall male, with once reddish hair that is turning grey, hazel eyes, and a quick smile? If you come up with a good name, you too could be an author.

Sunday School Answers

Regardless of what religion you follow, assuming that you believe in God, I'm sure there are basic things you are taught to do. I've often heard these referred to as "Sunday School Answers."

For example, if someone were to ask you what you can do to be more spiritual, the Sunday School answer would be, "Go to church, read your scriptures, say your prayers."

What about if you are going through a rough stretch in your life? Maybe you've lost your job, had a relationship end, had health issues, or any other number of things. If you ask a religious person what you should do, you may get the same Sunday School answers.

Lately, I've noticed some people ask questions in a religious setting, and before they allow people to respond, they'll say, "And I don't want the Sunday School answers."

To which I reply, "Why not?"

I honestly think that sometimes we make things more complicated than they need to be. There is something to be said for doing the basics consistently. That's true in many aspects of life. Do you want to lose weight? Eat right and exercise. Do you want to learn how to play a musical instrument? Practice. Do you find that you are tired all the time? Make sure you get enough rest.

For the example of losing weight, how many different diets are out there? How many of them contradict each other? But no one can deny that if you eat less and exercise, you'll lose weight.

There is a great story which I'm sure I'll mess up if I try to retell it verbatim, so I'll paraphrase.

A Native American young man has a vivid dream one night. He sees there are two wolves inside him—each fighting for dominance. The dream is powerful enough that he goes to see his wise grandfather to ask about it. The grandfather responds that every person has two wolves inside of them: one that seeks to be good, and one that seeks to be evil. The young man asks, "Which one will win?" The grandfather responds, "Whichever one you feed."

My point here is that by doing the basics in a consistent manner, we're feeding the proper wolf.

And so the next time someone responds to a question with the "Sunday School answers," I'm going to stand up and shout, "Halleluiah!"—or at the very least, smile and nod my head in agreement.

Questionable Christmas Lyrics

I love Christmas time. When I was young, it was such a magical experience. Watching the holiday specials like *Rudolf the Red-Nosed Reindeer* and *How the Grinch Stole Christmas* (the animated version) sparked my imagination. Our house was always decorated so nicely.

For many years, we had a real Christmas tree which was decorated with blinking multi-colored lights. These were especially cool because my brothers and I would make spaceships out of Legos and fly them around the tree, pretending the lights were lasers shooting at us.

In addition, it seemed that we always had Christmas music playing. To this day, during the holidays, I listen to Christmas music all the time. As I've gotten older and become more familiar with songs, I've raised my eyebrows at a few of the lyrics included in many of the popular songs. Granted, over time, meanings of certain words change, or things that were once considered acceptable are no longer so. Right away, I'll give a pass to the word "gay" which is present in several songs. Yes, before it meant "happy"—now, it has taken on a different meaning in the mainstream.

Some of these are humorous; some are serious.

I Saw Mommy Kissing Santa Claus: "What a laugh it would have been if Daddy had only seen Mommy kissing Santa Claus last night."

My take: If I saw my wife kissing another man, I wouldn't find it very funny.

Little Drummer Boy: "Shall I play for you (par-rum-ba-pum-pum) on my drum?"

My take: My big brother is an awesome drummer, so I'm familiar with how loud drummers can be. As a father who has raised four kids, I can't imagine a situation where someone playing the drums would make a baby happy.

Winter Wonderland: "We'll have lots of fun with Mr. Snowman, until the other kiddies knock him down."

My take: What kind of neighborhood do you live in where children will knock down your snowman?

It's Beginning to Look a Lot Like Christmas: "A pair of hop-a-long boots and a pistol that shoots is the wish of Barney and Ben."

My take: Do we really want to give loaded guns to some boys named Barney and Ben?

There's No Place Like Home For the Holidays: "From Atlantic to Pacific, gee the traffic is terrific."

My take: Some people have a different sense of what's terrific than I do.

Feed the World: "Well, tonight thank God it's them instead of you!"

My take: Ah, nothing shows the Christmas spirit like being thankful we're not someone else.

Baby It's Cold Outside: "Hey, what's in this drink?"

My take: This song is disturbing on several levels. I was debating over this line or "Think of my lifelong sorrow if you got pneumonia and died." In other words, he's telling her don't leave—not out of concern for her, but because of how it would impact him.

Santa Claus is Coming to Town: "He sees you when you're sleeping. He knows when you're awake."

My take: I don't like the idea of people watching me sleep. It's creepy.

Micromanaging

Have you ever been micromanaged, meaning that your boss tells you every little thing you have to do? They may often challenge or second-guess you any time you try to show your own initiative. How did this make you feel? Did you feel productive? Stifled? Appreciative that you didn't have to think for yourself? Something else I didn't note here?

I've been a manager for various companies over the last numerous years, and have taken my fair share of management classes.

One of the classes I really enjoyed explained how managers need to adjust their management style based on the person and the situation. And it makes total sense. Someone who is new to a job needs a lot of hand-holding until they are up to speed. Someone who has been in the role a long time and is productive basically needs support and trust, with little to no interference from their boss. And there are areas in between. Again, I didn't make this up—it is from a highly acclaimed management seminar (which I won't mention for legal reasons).

I once changed companies because I was being micromanaged to death. But it wasn't just me—it was everyone. In fact, when I left the company, several of my peers did the same. Why would you leave a job during such a harsh economic climate?

Well, everyone has the point where they say, "Enough is enough."

While I was debating whether or not to leave, I would think of those sayings or songs that talked about not giving up, keep on fighting the good fight and all that. So how do you answer when people tell you, "Ah, you couldn't handle it. You needed to hang in there and tough it out."

Here is the answer I came up with: I actually was the "noble warrior" by standing up and saying, "This environment is unproductive and unhealthy. Instead of surrendering who I am to become a pawn, or 'yes' man, I, as in me and myself, have decided to bravely leave this behind and venture into the unknown where I can better serve and be productive."

As for the company I left behind where everyone was being micromanaged? Well, what I found ironic was that they were the ones that paid me to attend the class about how everyone shouldn't be micromanaged. In other words, they paid me to realize that I was working for a company that didn't practice what it preached.

More Than One Way

My wife has an amazing ability to see something not for what it is, but what it can be. Over the course of our marriage, we've purchased four houses—each one a step up from where we had lived before. And in each case, we've left the house much better than we found it. The vast majority of the time, we did the work ourselves—or at least most of it. I can truly understand why they call it "sweat equity."

In our most recent house, there was an unfinished section above our two-car garage. It was actually one of the deciding factors for us to buy the house, because my wife and I knew we could turn it into living space. There is a term for such an area: FROG. It means Finished Room Over Garage. When I first heard the term, I wasn't enthralled by it. I didn't really relish the thought of spending time inside a frog.

As with most projects, there was more than one way to tackle it. Over the years, I've learned to follow my wife's lead and let her be the brains while I play the "dumb muscle." Aside from avoiding fights over what to do next, I'll have to admit the projects turn out much better. In other words, the project is her baby, and I'm there to change its diaper.

That isn't to say that I won't have an opinion on certain things time and again. However, I've learned that there are times when you say, "OK, this is your project, go for it." And then there are times when you say, "You know, I really feel strongly that perhaps we should try this instead."

This whole concept draws an eerie parallel to writing. While I was writing *The Hidden Sun*, I had several people read the story before I finally signed off on it. Each one had their own opinions on what they liked and didn't like, or thought could be better. Sometimes I felt that these suggestions were excellent and I incorporated them. Other times... not so much. But as a good friend of mine kept telling me, "Ultimately, it is your story."

From the reviews of *The Hidden Sun*, I've gotten enough feedback from people that I've decided that overall I've succeeded with what I was trying to do. Did everyone like it? Though a huge majority did, there were a few who didn't. And that's ok.

And then there was the time I took a Communications Law class for my degree. For our final paper, we had to choose a controversial topic and argue both sides, using court cases to back up our conclusions. I chose "Censorship on TV." There was a great quote from Max Headroom (look him up if you don't know who I am talking about) that went, "Ever wonder how successful censorship is on TV? Don't know the answer? Hmmmm...successful, isn't it?"

So I wrote the paper. We had to submit it to a fellow student as well as the teacher. The fellow student gave it high marks, saying I argued both sides well. The teacher? He gave me a "B." When I questioned him about the grade, his response was, "I don't think any of that filth should be on TV—you didn't argue enough to have it censored."

You Have to Have the Bad Days...

I was once told, "You have to have the bad days to appreciate the good days."

While that makes sense, it's often cold comfort when you are having one of those "bad" days. I remember one of those bad days.

It started innocently enough. I was running through my emails and such. I noticed someone had posted a review on my book *The Hidden Sun*. And it was the worst review I've ever received. You know you're in trouble when the reviewer uses the word "whilst" in the first few words.

Her biggest two complaints were this: First, I used contractions in the book. She said that's a "big no-no" in English literature. Wait. What? I'd never heard that before.

I checked with some of my author friends. They hadn't heard of it either. One author said that at one point in time she had a professor mention that, but it was no longer a rule.

The second thing that bugged her was that the book read like "a TV show or movie script," meaning that I write in smaller scenes, and use several characters to tell an overall story. Well, you know what? That was intentional. And frankly, it's one of the things many people have liked about it.

Lastly, at the end of her review, she included two big "spoilers." Talk about a no-no!

I know it shouldn't bother me, mainly because the reviewer was obviously from la-la land, but it did.

Intellectually, I recognized I was in a bad mood. Yet I couldn't seem to shake off the feeling of being upset. I'm experienced enough in life to realize that often *time* is the only thing that will allow my emotions to settle down.

By dinner, I was fairly calm. My wife had taken my oldest two daughters shopping for school supplies. I had to run some errands with my youngest two daughters. Normally we eat dinner as a family, but on that day, we ate it on the run. My two youngest and I went to KFC.

The girls wanted to try the new chicken bites, so I bought a 10 piece for them to share. After waiting for about 15 minutes, my order number was called. I went to the front and the employee told me, "We are all out of chicken bites." She even made a slashing motion across her neck to emphasize her point. "I can give you a couple of pieces of chicken instead."

My daughters aren't big fans of chicken on the bone. I looked at the menu board and then at my receipt. They had chicken strips, 3 for $3.99. I had paid $4.49 for 10 bites. I said, "Tell you what, give me 4 strips, and we'll call it even."

She shook her head violently. "I'll only do three."

Now, keep in mind, I was still coming down from a pretty bad day. It would have been easy for me to blow up at her. Instead, I took a deep breath and in a calm voice said, "I paid $4.49 for the bites. You're offering me something worth $3.99."

Her response? "But when you add tax, $3.99 gets close to $4.49!"

I was flabbergasted. Still, I kept it together—somehow. "I paid $4.49 *before* tax. And frankly, you sold me something you didn't have—and you've kept us waiting quite a while. Honestly, you should be doing whatever you can to make it right, not trying to bargain with me."

At that point, she gave me the stink eye and said she would have to get a manager. I could see the employee go talk to him. She was flapping her arms in disgust and also pointing at me. I didn't hear what the manager said to her, but he came over and said, "I'm so sorry. Of course you can have 4 strips. Can I get you a free side as well for your trouble?" I declined on the side, but thanked him.

Later that night, I thought about that employee at KFC. Part of me wondered if something hadn't happened to her earlier in the day to put her in a bad mood. It didn't excuse her actions, but at least I could relate.

R.I.P. Cursive

I took the GRE test once. If you aren't sure what that is, it's like the SAT for graduate school. I studied very hard for a week and then took it on Friday. When I was done, it felt like I'd stubbed my toe, only instead of my toe, it was my brain.

I can't really disclose too much information about the GRE. They're super secretive about that. I can say the test took about four hours and consisted of essays, math questions, and English questions. Each section was timed—so you had to pace yourself on figuring out the answers or you'd run out of time. Aside from that, I can't say much about it. I had to sign a form promising my first born if I revealed too much—ok, maybe not my first born, but you get the idea.

On the form where I promised to not share the answers with the world, there was a section where I had to re-write a paragraph stating just that. When this was explained to me by the nice man at the desk, he underlined the part of the directions that said DO NOT PRINT. This meant I was to write the paragraph in cursive.

Cursive? Really?

The only thing I use cursive for is to sign my name. When I print anything, it's in all capital letters—and it's a mess.

I blame my poor handwriting on two things: first, college. This may sound strange, but it's true. When taking notes in class, I would write as fast as I could and I wasn't concerned about how it looked because I was the only one who needed to decipher the mess. Second, working as a TV director. Directors mark scripts, making notes and such. During live programs, you have precious little time, so speed trumps neatness.

But back to cursive.

I had arrived early for the GRE test, so I had plenty of time to fill out the forms. I did my best to remember how to make all the letters in cursive—but frankly, I didn't remember some of them. I dare say it took me twice as long to copy the paragraph in cursive as it would have by printing it. Thank goodness that wasn't part of the graded test.

I remember my kids saying how cursive is being phased out of the school systems. I'm sure some traditionalists are freaking out about that. I did some digging and came across an interesting article.

One interesting fact I learned was that "44 states no longer mandate teaching cursive in the classrooms. Of those 44, two of them—Indiana and Hawaii— have taken it out of the curriculum completely."

Why is that? Well, it states that "Computers in the classroom have left little time for educators to teach print, cursive, and typing. Something had to give. It certainly wasn't going to be math or science. Instead, it's cursive."

From my point of view, cursive is a dying art form. During my lifetime I've seen it become less and less prevalent. As I stated before, I don't use it—and until the GRE, I hadn't missed it.

Mixing It Up with the Fuzz

Have you ever spoken to someone who acts like they don't believe anything you say? If you have, then you understand how frustrating it can be, especially when you are telling the truth. If you haven't, where do you live? I want to live there.

Sadly, the police officers I've had to deal with seem to assume I'm lying. I can understand that to a point. I'm sure they get lied to a lot of the time because people don't want to get in trouble. If that's the majority of what they deal with, I can see how they would tend to be skeptical of what they hear.

I respect police officers. They don't have an easy job. I feel comforted that I can call 911 and they'll come rushing to my aid. At the same time, I don't appreciate being assumed guilty until I can prove my innocence.

One day I was driving down a side road and came to a "checkpoint" set up by the police. They were seeing if drivers had their licenses and that their registrations were up to date. Why they were doing it, I don't know. It's not like I live in a crime-ridden area. My town is a great place to raise a family and is generally quiet.

When it was my turn to be "inspected" by the police, I had my driver's license ready. I rolled down my window and handed it to the officer. He looked over the license very carefully, double checking that I looked like me. (Which, in my opinion, I do.)

He gave me back my license and said, "I need to check the tags on your license plate." The officer walked to the back of my car, looked for a moment and then came back to my window.

"Your plates expire today," he said.

"No, they don't," I said. "I put the new sticker on just a few weeks ago."

"You're wrong! They expire today," he said forcefully.

I was taken back by how insistent he was. "Officer, go take a look again. I know my tags are up to date," I said.

"I checked already," he said.

(Okay, even I'll admit I was a bit out of line with this next part.) "Well, go check it again and you'll see I'm right," I said, matching his tone.

"Show me your registration," he said gruffly.

"Fine!" I said, exasperated. While I reached for it, I said, "I don't understand why you just won't go double check. It's not like I'm going to try to run away with all these other police around."

By this time, another police officer came over to my car.

"Is there a problem?" he asked.

"Yeah," I said. "This officer is insisting my plates are about to expire, when I know they're fine.

He won't go double check and is bordering on harassment."

I handed my registration to the second officer. The first officer was about to say something, but was silenced by a look from the second officer. Reviewing my registration, the second officer saw it was indeed up to date.

"One moment," he said.

He motioned for the first officer to follow him behind my car. I couldn't hear what they were saying, but I saw the second officer point to what I assumed was my license plate. He returned a moment later.

"Your tags are fine," he said.

Humiliation as a Motivator

I'm not a big fan of seeing someone get yelled at in public. I'm even less of a fan of seeing someone in authority disciplining one of their subordinates in front of their peers. I guess there can be a case made for that, though a lame one.

When I have had to put someone on "corrective action" (the politically correct term), I made it a point to do it one-on-one, in a setting away from their siblings or co-workers. One downside: when the person being "corrected" said, "It's not fair! No one else is getting in trouble!" My response was, "How do you know? Is there anyone else here watching this discussion? No? Then they have no idea. The only way they'll know is if *you* tell them."

This next story is not one of my finer moments, but it's worth sharing to demonstrate my point.

When I was in the 10th grade, I had a math teacher who would go student to student to collect their homework. And if you didn't have it, she'd make you explain why to the whole class.

I was always good at completing my homework. After I finished it, I'd fold the paper in half and put it in my math book. Any corrected homework would also go back into the math book so I could review it for the next test.

At my house, I often did my homework on the couch. Next to the couch were the newspapers we had for the week. I was also a paper carrier along with my siblings during this time, so we always had extra newspapers hanging around.

One night, I finished my homework, put my math book on the couch and went to bed. (Yeah, I should have put the book away, I know.) The next morning, I discovered that our two poodles had been running around the house and knocked my math book right into the pile of newspapers. My assignments were all mixed up in the newspapers, and of course, I was running late, so I grabbed what I could and took off to school.

When I arrived at my math class, I realized that my homework from the night before was missing. I was mortified! I didn't want to have to explain to the teacher what happened in front of the class. But sure enough, she did her rounds. When she got to me, she asked, "Where's your homework?"

I started to explain by saying, "Well, you see, we have these two dogs..." Before I could say anything else, she interrupted me. "Oh, I see. Your dog ate your homework. Is that it?"

Everyone in the class started laughing...at me. I tried to tell her no, and wanted to tell her what really happened, but she cut me off by saying, "I can't believe you really tried to use that lame excuse." She then moved on to the next student.

For the next several classes, when I walked in, she would make some sort of comment about my dogs and that I should keep my "tasty" homework away from them.

My response? I stopped going to that class. There were only a few more days in the semester. After that, I wouldn't have to see her again. I ended up getting a "D" in the class from not taking the final exam. As I look back on it, I learned a lot from that teacher, but it wasn't about math.

Expected to Volunteer

I spent a few years working in the banking industry. When I first started, I was impressed that we were given paid time to do volunteer work in the community. Granted, we had to volunteer for certain types of qualified activities, but still, I was happy the company would be willing to do that.

Every so often we'd get notifications of certain events the bank was sponsoring and they would ask for volunteers. Over time, the paid time allowed to do volunteer work was reduced and the bank sponsored events moved from being voluntary to an expectation—especially for salaried managers. Regardless of what volunteer activity was completed, it needed to be documented.

One activity was held on a Sunday. It conflicted with my church obligations. I remember getting a call from my district manager asking me why my name wasn't on the list of volunteers from my branch—I was the manager, after all. I explained that I had a previous commitment to my church. His response was, "This is the biggest event we do all year! How will it look if I don't have all my managers there?" I went on to explain that I had already made a commitment to my church at that time. He responded, "It's just this one Sunday! Your God will understand."

I didn't back down and I kept my commitment to my Heavenly Father. To me, jobs come and go, but it's the eternal things that matter the most.

Some time later, I was studying one of the many rules and regulations we needed to follow as bankers. One of them is something called the "Community Reinvestment Act" (or CRA). The Community Reinvestment Act was passed in 1977 as a federal law designed to encourage commercial banks and savings associations to help meet the needs of borrowers in all segments of their communities, including low- and moderate-income neighborhoods.

Banks are audited time and again to make sure they are following this act. What is one thing banks can do to make sure they will do well in these audits? Simple: have proof that the bank is doing "qualified" volunteer work.

So in the end, the bank leaders weren't paying us to do volunteer work or holding these volunteer events out of the kindness of their hearts. It was all part of the plan to make sure they were able to pass the CRA audits.

To be fair, a lot of people in the community benefited from these volunteer activities. And I know that whenever I give service to another, I feel good inside—so I can only imagine there were many other employees that felt the same way.

But the question lingers: how sincere are the bank's motives to do volunteer work when they are basically forced to do it?

What Nickname Would You Give
Someone Named Nick?

When my wife and I were newlyweds, I got a call from her one night telling me that we were "going to have an addition to the family." I was in shock! I was going to be a dad! Or at least that's what I thought until she continued, "I'm bringing home a puppy!"

She brings home this little fluff ball—a terrier / poodle mix, also known as a terri-poo. This cute little puppy was smaller than my shoe, and promised not to be much bigger as he grew.

Since my wife made the executive decision to add to the family, she agreed I could name him. I looked at this puppy and thought, "This little dog is going to need a big name." My selection? Armageddon.

Now Armageddon is a bit of a mouthful, so a nickname was needed. A traditional nickname would be "Army," but we didn't like that. So I borrowed the "g" further down in the name and ta-da! The nickname "Argy" was born. (Also known as "Argy Dargy.")

I've always found it interesting to find out how someone has gotten a nickname, even though no one can always explain why they "stick."

There are many strange nicknames that have stuck in my family. My oldest sister? Fred. (My mother was much dismayed that her only daughter was given a boy's nickname.) My big brother's name is Buck. Why Fred and Buck? I don't know.

My little brother? Hose, short for "hoser," as in a term from the 80's meaning "dork, goofy head, and silly pants." If you had ever met my little brother back then, you'd know why.

To this day, I'll call him that, and my kids affectionately call him "Uncle Hose."

My kids have had all sorts of nicknames over the years, but none more interesting than my third child, who for the first few years of her life was "Ba-boo." She was an early walker, which also meant she fell a lot. When she would fall, she'd look up at us like, "Am I ok?" We'd respond "bonk-a-boo!" in a light, happy voice, letting her know she was fine. However, she would fall so often, over time we shortened it to "Ba-boo!" There was even a time when she wouldn't answer to her given name—only to Ba-boo (though if we call her that now, she gives us the evil eye.)

Growing up, I never really liked my middle name. It came from my grandfather, who I thought was cool, but "Lloyd" sounded so old-fashioned. My little brother caught on to this fact and would call me Lloyd every chance he could get. (He still calls me that to this day.)

But then it came time to pick a pseudonym, or pen name, for my books. My given name, Jason Morgan, is way too common (I went to high school with another Jason Morgan). There is also a character on General Hospital with the same name. I also wanted the pseudonym to be reflective of the real me, so J. Lloyd Morgan was born.

Lose Half Your Weight!
(By Using the Metric System)

I once took a trip to Ontario, Canada for business. While there, I watched a local newscast. It was February, and when the weatherman came on, he said the high was going to be negative 2 degrees. Yikes! However, that was using the metric system. As an American, I'll admit I was a bit clueless about what that meant to me. I did some digging and found out that meant it was going to be 21 degrees Fahrenheit. That's still cold, but not negative 2 degrees cold.

It was also trippy to see speed limit signs that said 100 km/h. At first I thought, "Wow! These people can really go fast up here." It turns out that 100 km/h is about 62 miles per hour.

I remember in junior high learning about the metric system. What struck me was how logical it was. Though it was different than what I was used to, it made sense.

For giggles, ask 10 people how many feet are in a mile. I'll bet you a nickel most will say, "I don't have any idea." (The answer is 5,280 feet in a mile.) If you go to Canada and ask 10 people how many meters are in a kilometer, I'm sure you're going to get the right answer. Heck, they may tease you and ask you, "What's next? Are you going to ask me how many minutes are in an hour?"

Aside from the USA, Burma (Myanmar), Liberia, and Antarctica are using different systems other than metric.

I could go into all of the history of why the USA hasn't switched, but there are better, more detailed articles on the subject you can read if you really want to know.

If I were to guess why we haven't switched, it would be a combination of a few things.

First, it would cost a boatload of money to switch all the signs.

Second, we're used to it. In general, people don't like change—especially to things that are so commonplace. (My whole adult life I've been 6'3." What if I had to tell people I was now 191 cm? I'd sound like a giant! On the other hand, my weight number would be cut in more than half, so that could be a good thing…)

Third, I believe it might be pride. I'm proud to be an American. I'm not always proud of what the government does, but that's a different story.

In my opinion, I be a lot of Americans don't see the need to change because we're America—people should change to us. Right?

Survey says…

I'm always a bit leery of information based on a "recent survey." There are so many factors involved in any sort of survey that if they aren't done correctly, the results can be misleading.

Case in point: if I were to take a survey of the people under the age of 18 that are currently in my house, 100% of them would be female. In addition, all of them would be members of the Church of Jesus Christ of Latter-day Saints. But wait! There's more! All of them were born in the USA. Using this data, I could say, "In a recent survey, all females under the age of 18 born in the USA are LDS."

Often there are surveys that contradict each other. I can't help believe that some of the surveys are biased based on what the person conducting the survey is hoping to prove.

Keeping all this in mind, I came across a recent story that claims, "Working More Than 40 Hours a Week is Useless." That's a pretty big claim—and frankly a bit misleading.

Don't get me wrong, I'm in total agreement that the work week should be kept at 40 hours a week. However, while I agree with parts of the story, my reasons are somewhat different.

The story claims that "According to a handful of studies, consistently clocking over 40 hours a week just makes you unproductive (and very, very tired)."

Also, "What these studies showed, over and over, was that industrial workers have eight good, reliable hours a day in them. On average, you get no more widgets out of a ten-hour day than you do out of an eight-hour day."

I've stated in other stories my disdain for companies that abuse the "exempt" laws for employees. Basically, if you are considered to be an "exempt" employee (which to over-simplify it means you are paid a salary) you don't have to get paid overtime if you work more than 40 hours. It's been my experience that larger companies equate the number of hours you spend at work to how dedicated an employee you are. To that I say: hogwash!

I had a boss that claimed to work from 7 am to 7 pm every day. However, he would often be gone for large chunks of time during the middle of the day. Sometimes he was getting his hair cut. Sometimes he was getting his car tuned up. Sometimes he was at the doctor. Now, I don't begrudge him having to do these things. But it does help support my position for a 40 hour work week: work / life balance.

To me, a bigger argument for a 40 hour work week is to have a work / life balance. The best employees I've had were those that were actively involved in their family / church / community / hobbies or any of those in combination. They were happier at work, which made them more productive.

We'd get better work done in 8 hours than during a 10 or 12 hour shift.

I'll admit there are times that working more than 40 hours may be needed time and again—but that should be the exception and not the rule.

A Saint Patrick's Day Story

In honor of that holiday that has become yet another reason to get plastered, here is my favorite Saint Patrick's Day story:

Two men are sitting at a bar, celebrating Saint Patrick's Day. One of them turns to the other and says, "You look familiar for some reason. Do I know ya?"

The other man responds, "Ya know, ya look familiar to me too. Where ya from?"

"I'm from North Clover," the first man says.

"No foolin'! I'm from North Clover too! Where did ya go to school?"

"I went to Saint Mary's."

The second man looks shocked. "No foolin'! I went to Saint Mary's too! Who was your teacher?"

"Her name was Sister Constance. I swear I still have bruises on my knuckles from her ruler."

Examining his own hands, the second man says, "Oh, aye! I still remember that ruler!"

"We must have gone to school together! When did you go?" the first man asks.

As the second man starts to count on his fingers to figure out how long ago it was, the owner of the tavern comes up to the bartender and says, "All right then, lad, I think the O'Dooly twins have had enough to drink."

These Are the Good Old Days

When one of my daughters was eleven-years-old, she mentioned at dinner one night, "I remember the good old days when…" She then went on to talk about a particular time when she was playing with her cousins. What made this really cute was that we were, at that moment, having dinner with these same cousins. After listening to her for a moment, I said, "Do you realize that in a few years *these* will be the good old days?" She looked at me as if I had just uttered the most profound thing she'd ever heard.

It reminded me of a day when I was a senior at BYU. I was walking from one class to another with some classmates. It was cold. It was snowy. We had just left a class where we had been given a huge assignment. No doubt, the class we were headed to would add even more to our workload. It seemed like we had been going to school forever, and even though we were in our last year, the end seemed far away. I remember mentioning to my classmates, "You do realize that right here, right now, these are the good old college days." Once again, the response was one of "Are you crazy?"

On Monday nights we spend time together as a family. It's called family home evening. One thing we like to do is watch videos of when the children were younger. At the time we shot these videos, I was worn out from our first three kids being so close in age (they were each born about 18 months apart). When I watch the videos and see how cute and fun they were, I miss it. I'm sure at the time I would never have thought I'd say that.

Who is to Blame?

"Everyone talks about the weather, but no one does anything about it." I've always loved that saying. Why does everyone talk about the weather? It is something that impacts everyone—the sun doesn't shine only on certain races, genders, or social classes. The weather is an equal opportunity event.

Something else that people discuss but rarely do anything about is ethics. Hang on! Don't let your eyes gloss over just yet. Give yourself a chance to think about this for a moment.

One of the classes I took in college was "Values and Ethics." There was one story in particular which I recall quite well: The Ring of Gyges. It was a story told in *Plato's Republic*. Basically, the ring of Gyges had the ability to turn the owner invisible at will. The question the story asked was, "Would a typical person be moral if he didn't have to fear the consequences of his actions?"

But what if you had another type of power, aside from turning invisible, which made you feel like you didn't have to worry about the consequences of your actions? "Like what?" you may ask. Oh, I don't know—have you read the news in, let's say, the last 100 years? How many public figures have been "caught" for doing something wrong and ended up going to jail? When I lived in Connecticut, the governor was caught taking bribes—so was the mayor of Bridgeport. Both went to jail.

Why would they do these illegal activities? Did they honestly feel that with their power they could do what they wanted, and therefore didn't care if it was "right" or not? Or was it because of the pressures around them?

In the book *Utopia*, Sir Thomas Moore basically said, "If the leaders don't provide the common people with the means to support themselves, and the people are forced to do whatever they can to survive, whether or not it is considered legal or ethical, it is the leaders that are to blame."

Sadly, I've seen this happen in corporate America—and it is getting worse. Bosses are making more demands on employees because with the high unemployment rate, people are willing to do just about anything to keep their jobs. Some of them are even willing to do things that by their very definition are unethical, but they see it as their only way to survive. If the so-called "leaders" of a company are making such high demands that the only way some people can truly compete is by bending the ethical rules, who is truly at fault? Plus, if all you hear from the leaders is "results, results, results!" and ethics is only discussed after someone is "caught," you have to wonder—where is the focus?

Don't misunderstand me. I believe everyone controls their own choices. But consider this: imagine you had children at home who were starving. You go look for food, and spot a loaf of bread at the same time three other people do. All of you need it. What would you do to ensure you got that loaf of bread? Would you fight them for it? Steal? Kill?

At one of my jobs, we had to take a very long and intense class about ethics. At the end of the session, the teacher summed it up with two sentences.

#1: "Just because it's legal, doesn't make it ethical."
 #2: "Treat others the way you want to be treated."

Hmmm. I know I've heard that second statement somewhere else before …

Pulling Your Punches

"Well, duh! It was ground this morning."

Does that sentence make any sense to you? It really shouldn't. It's a punch line for a joke. So why did I write the punch line first? To prove a point.

The joke starts like this: A woman walks into a coffee shop. She goes there quite often and knows all the workers by name. However, today she goes in and there is a new employee. The young man seems nice enough, but doesn't really appear to know what he is doing. The woman talks with the young worker for a moment and finds out it is his first day, and his trainer went home sick earlier. She orders her regular drink and the young man looks confused for a moment but then goes about his work. In the meantime, the woman gets a call on her cell phone. The young man comes back a little bit later with the coffee cup. The woman pays him, still distracted while on the phone. While exiting the store, she takes a sip and then promptly spits it out. She spins around and says to the worker, "This coffee tastes like mud!" (Now read the first line of the story again.)

There are certain TV shows I watch and never miss an episode. For almost all of these shows, I make it a point never to watch the following week's previews. Why? Because most of the time, they give too much away! Movie previews (AKA trailers) are often the worst offenders. There are countless times

I've been watching a movie and during a tense moment I've thought, "OK, based on the previews, I know what is going to happen."

It ruins the experience.

Or how about the times when there is something shown in a movie preview that never ends up in the movie? Let me get this straight—the scene is good enough for the preview to entice people to see the movie, but not good enough for the movie itself?

I'm not sure if the people in charge of the previews think the general public have no long term memories, but why include shots of the final part of the movie in the previews?

It's actually rather insulting.

In the end, I'm writing an open letter to the preview makers: Make the previews interesting without ruining the movie / TV show / book. Give your audience some credit.

Give Me a 10!

First off, I'm all in favor of treating people nicely. You know, the whole golden rule concept. There are certain establishments that are considered "service" businesses.

The first one that comes to my mind is restaurants. My wife and I classify restaurants in two different ways: fast food and sit down. The difference? With sit down, you are expected to give a tip at the end of your meal based on the service.

I'll admit that I tend to tip on the generous side because I understand how hard they are working.

Once in a while, the service will be really good—to the point where I'll seek out a manager to compliment the employee. On the other hand, if the service is poor, I'll just give them a lower tip and leave it at that.

I heard of a story where a guy was so upset at the service that on the receipt under "tip" he wrote, "-$2.00! The service was terrible!"

However, I'm seeing a trend where the focus on customer service is getting out of hand. I understand businesses are doing whatever they can to find an edge. One of the ways they do this is to provide excellent customer service. Yet I disagree with how they are going about it.

Recently, I took my car into the dealership to have the oil changed. I had a coupon. I was treated very well, and they did a wonderful job. Not only did they give my car an oil change, but they also washed it and vacuumed the inside.

When it came time to pay, the service rep was very nice and explained what he had done. That took about one minute. For the next two minutes, he explained how I'd be getting a call about my service experience. He showed me their banner they had "won" for the best service in the region. He explained how if I scored them lower than a "10" on *any* rating, they would fail.

Over the next couple of days, I received a call from the dealership reminding me to give them all 10s on the survey. I got an email reminding me. When we got the call, we gave them all 10s—which I would have done anyway. They did a great job.

So what is my point? Here's a crazy idea. Stop the completely unfair rating systems.

Instead of spending time and money telling me and reminding me how great the service was, spend it on, oh I don't know…service?

What If?

As a child, I would often ask questions that began with "What if …?" Now, I'm sure some of these questions were fairly valid, like, "What if I tried to sleep with a baseball cap on?" or "What if I put orange juice in my cereal instead of milk?" (Side note: I actually tried that with a bowl of Cap'n Crunch once. The experience was something I'd rather not repeat.)

But then I would ask my mom questions like, "What if the grass was purple instead of green?" or "What if I could jump so high that I could jump over the house?"

How would you respond if your child asked such questions? I'm sure I'd come up with some sort of smart-alecky answer like, "Well, let me throw you over the house and tell me how that works out for you." Granted, that wouldn't be the best way I could answer the question.

I've come to realize that the "what if" questions were just my little mind trying to figure out the world around me. My curiosity would sometimes get me into trouble, like discovering what would happen when you mix vinegar with baking soda—but not before you put food coloring in the vinegar to make it purple. The result was…messy.

However, once in a while I would put my "what if" mind to other, less destructive uses. In the

80's, we had an Atari game system. There was one game—I forget the name of it—where you would play with a partner. The goal was to run through a castle type of maze to gather treasure and avoid getting touched by the monsters. If you got touched by a monster, your health would go down. But not to worry, if your partner touched you, your health would go back up.

The tricky part was finding a partner who could stay close to you pretty much at all times. It wasn't easy. So, using my "what if" mind, I took apart a couple of the controllers and combined them so one controller was hooked to two wires that went into the gaming system. The result? Whenever I moved the controller, both of the little characters would move together in perfect sync. Needless to say, I broke every record in that game.

But my "what if" mind didn't stop as a child. It's still there, asking all sorts of questions. How do you feed such an insatiable beast? You become a writer! However, I find as I write, my characters are the ones asking, "What if…?"

One Way to Fix Squeaky Breaks

A little part of me died the day we bought our first minivan. It was one of those moments in my life when I realized that I had crossed over into full-fledged parenting. No longer would the family vehicle be without a sliding door. It was odd to be able to walk around inside. For my kids? It was like a play land.

A few years came and went and it was time for a new minivan. The dealer we went to was, well, persistent. They made an offer on the van we owned, and really low balled us on it. After talking back and forth a bit, my wife and I got up and left. It was obvious that we were not going to get what we were looking for.

Several days went by and we got a call from the salesman. He said they had found a buyer for our old van and were able to offer us a much higher trade-in. In addition, they included an 8 year, 80,000 mile bumper to bumper warranty as part of the deal. Though we were a bit put off that it took us walking out on them to get a good deal, we accepted.

Over the years, the van would have issues now and again. So we'd take it into the dealer, warranty in hand, and tell them what was wrong. Without going into a lot of details on the various issues, it seemed like every time we took it in, they found something else wrong with it as well. On at least a couple occasions, we had to take the van back more than once to get them to fix it right.

One summer, the brakes started acting up. They weren't part of the bumper to bumper warranty, but we took it to the dealership nonetheless, sure that they would find something wrong in addition (which they did) that we could get fixed under the warranty. So we got new brakes.

It was at that point that the breaks started squeaking. It wasn't too bad at first, but it continued to get worse. Finally, we took the van back to the dealership a few months later to have them check it out. The answer we got? That the brake shoes had "glazed" over and had ruined the rotors. How do brake shoes get glazed over? According to the tech, it was because we had been riding them too hard and / or braking too quickly. Again, we had had this van for seven years, and only *now* we were having this problem? If that was truly the case, wouldn't it have happened earlier?

The solution? All new brakes, including new rotors. Ug.

And that solved the issue, right? No—not so much. The brakes were now squeaking as badly as ever. So a month later we took the van back—again. What was the problem? The shoes were glazed over again. The tech insisted it was operator error. But they agreed to fix the issue for free since we had just had them done a month previous.

They put on new shoes and pads and resurfaced the rotors—rotors that were new just a month ago. And yes, they found something else wrong with the car as well at the same time—but it was unrelated to the brakes.

The dilemma we faced was that our warranty was about to expire. We had lost total confidence in this dealership. I went as far as to call the head service guy to nicely express my concern. When we talked about the squeaky brakes, his answer was this: "They have changed the material the pads are made from, so yeah, they squeak. The way to get them to stop is to brake a bit harder now and again."

When I pointed out that braking hard is what the tech said was causing the glazing issue, the head service guy said, "Well, don't overdo it."

For a moment there, I was reminded of the advice Ralphie from *The Simpsons* was given by his father: "Remember, son, if your nose starts to bleed, it's because you are picking it too much—or not enough."

My wife was especially upset with this whole ordeal—and she had every right to be. What problem would they find next? How much was it going to cost us once the warranty ended? For those that don't know my wife, she is amazingly patient (she has to be, she's married to me). How were we going to fix these squeaky breaks? Then the answer came to us:

simple—we were going to trade in our old van for a new one—from a different dealership.

And that we did. On the way home, I turned off the radio and asked my wife as we were slowing down, "Do you hear that?"

Knowing the way I think, she smiled and said, "Yes. That's the sound of breaks not squeaking."

Are Some Corporations a Form of Religion?

I've worked with several different types of companies over the years. Some were small, some were huge. There are advantages to both.

I enjoyed working for a small company in Idaho. It had a family feel to it and I honestly felt like the management knew me and cared about what I did. The down side was that the pay was pretty low and the benefits weren't all that great.

I went to work for bigger companies after that, mainly for the benefits. My wife and I were at that stage where we were having kids and wanted to have better benefits.

A common trait of all these larger businesses was something called "orientation." The new hires sat in a room and learned about the history of the company, its leaders, and the company goals. Over time, these orientations also included the company's "core values," sometimes called "vision and values."

While I was working for one company a few years back, it was taken over by an even larger company.

I was a manager at the time and had to attend a two day course to learn about our new "masters."

I remember a video being shown at the start of the first day. It was a "day in the life" of a typical manager. It started out with, "This is Bob. He's a manager. He loves fishing, hiking, traveling, and spending time with his family." We were shown scenes of Bob doing these activities. "Here is what Bob does during a typical day." From there, it outlined a day that started around 7:00 am and ended after 8:00 pm. In addition, "Bob" works half days on Saturdays.

I thought, "How does Bob do any of the activities he likes when he is working so much?"

Another video showed testimonials of various employees gushing about how much they loved working for the company and why. Over the next two days, we learned how the new company did business. In the end, our vacation time was reduced dramatically, we lost two paid holidays, our bonus opportunities were cut in half, and so on. Yet the whole time this information was told to us, we were instructed that as managers we needed to believe in these changes so that our employees would as well.

Over the next few weeks, our regional managers were replaced with people from the new company. When these new people spoke of the company, they did so almost reverently. It was clear that this new company culture was based on doing what you were told and not to question things.

We were given a list of the company's "vision, mission, and values" that we were supposed to memorize and put into practice with our employees. However, I found that these vision, mission, and values were wonderful in concept, but during practical, everyday application, the company would often bend, twist, and even break them.

For example, one of the values was based on integrity. However, our leaders decided to have a blitz to see how many sales we could get in one day. Their plan? For two weeks we were supposed to sell all we could, but only on paper. We wouldn't enter the sales into the computer until that one day. There was even a memo stating we needed to come in really early and stay late that day to enter in all the sales.

This caused me great concern. I went to my immediate supervisor. Her answer? "This is the way things are done. Do as you're told." I felt badly enough about this that I reported it to the ethics line set up by the company.

In the end, the leaders got in trouble—but not nearly as much as I did. Because I'd gone to my supervisor first, as I should have, it was made known that I was probably the one who had called the ethics line—even though it was supposed to be anonymous.

Here is what I learned: I applaud that large companies have defined visions and values, but not if they don't practice what they preach. For me, religion is a very personal thing that helps guide my actions and the decisions I make. It gives me hope. It gives me a feeling of peace. It gives me a desire to be a better person. Sure, there are "rules" to follow, but I've found that they are designed to build me up.

As devoted as I am to my faith, I've met people with that same amount of devotion to the company they work for. I could write pages and pages of the differences, but there is one perfect example that sums it up.

I knew a lady who had worked for a company her whole adult life. She had worked her way up the ladder. She came to work early. She stayed late. She ate lunches at her desk. On the weekends, she would volunteer to do company sponsored events. However, when times got tough, her position was eliminated. In the end, all her hard work and devotion didn't matter to the company. I spoke to her a few weeks after that. She had a lost look in her eyes.

She said, "That job was everything to me. I don't know what to believe in now."

Are Scars Really Scary?

I've been cut on more than one occasion. Usually it's from doing some sort of work gone wrong, and almost always some sort of physical reminder is left behind. It seems the older I get, the more scars I collect.

Most of my scars came from my days in college when I was working at a grocery store. We would use box cutters, which are basically razor blades encased in a metal shell with the tip of the blade sticking out. If you were not paying attention, the result could be unpleasant.

I have a pretty decent scar on my left thumb from when I worked in the meat department. Let me just say that the knives in the meat department are rather sharp. One little slip and "Oops, there goes part of my thumb."

Some of my scars were not self-inflicted. When I was around ten-years-old or so, we learned that if you threw metal tipped darts at the asphalt street when it was dark, it could sometimes cause a visible spark. We also learned you could freak people out by throwing the darts near their feet. One of the neighbor boys turned out to be a pretty bad aim because one of his throws ended up stuck into my right shin.

Sometimes scars are from accidents when doing something nice for someone else. We had a foster brother when I was younger. I must have been four or five at the time. He was awesome. He loved to play with us. One thing we liked to do was have him grab us by our ankles and swing us around. He was swinging me one day and misjudged how close I was to a corner of the wall. I remember the trip to the hospital.

I have the scar on my forehead as a reminder.

What got me thinking about this subject was something I noticed when I was on a date with my wife. As we were holding hands, I noticed that she, too, had a few scars that were not there when we first were married.

These could have come from any number of projects she and I have tackled over the years (but that's a whole different story). Here is one I remember: I was on the computer, probably writing or re-writing something, when I heard my wife call my name from the kitchen. She didn't use that tone of voice very often, and usually only when something significant had happened (like when her water broke during her last pregnancy).

In this case, she had been washing the dishes and a glass pie plate had broken in half, and in the process, cut a pretty deep slice into her thumb. She couldn't bring herself to look at it. I sat her down, and calmly I had her lift her other hand so I could see the cut. When I saw bone, I figured we'd better get to the hospital. It all turned out fine, but the scar remains.

Think about this: scars come from something that at the time can cause quite a "scare"—which is just the word "scar" with an "e" at the end. When I figured this out, my mind started playing, as it tends to do, and I thought to myself, "Self, what if I were to move the 's' from the beginning of 'scare' to the end of the word?" I'd end up with 'cares'. (My mind does stuff like that from time to time.)

After figuring that out, when I look again at my wife's hands, I don't see scars. Instead, I see evidence of how much she "cares" for me and our family.

The New Math

There's that old joke that algebra could one day save your life. With my imagination, when I was a student I'd daydream of a situation where a bomb was going to blow up unless I solved this complex equation using all sorts of letters and symbols. How that would keep a bomb from blowing up, I'm not sure.

The honest fact is that unless you use something on a regular basis, you tend to forget it. Some may say this is a perfect argument for not getting an education—that most things you learn, you won't use. I'll say that is somewhat of a valid point, with one major exception:

Learning helps you learn to learn.

Granted, that may seem like the most obvious statement in the world. But stuff is changing around us so much, we are constantly having to learn new things.

At BYU, I learned how to direct TV programs. At the time, we used the latest technology. We had this big video switcher that looked like the control board on the Death Star.

It had lots of buttons and levers and dials and such. Over time, technology changed—things became more computer based. One summer, we went back to Utah for a visit. We stopped by BYU. I found the old studio where I had spent so many hours. It was stripped bare. I have no doubt that all that equipment was replaced by the newest technology somewhere else on campus.

So what was the point of me learning something that would change? Well, for starters, the concepts behind directing haven't really changed. The correct video still needs to be played at the right moment. The anchors need to know which camera to look at and when. The director needs the ability to multitask while several people are talking to him or her at the same time. In other words, the human elements haven't changed.

But in addition, learning how all that equipment worked helped me develop the strategies and habits to be able to become proficient at something new. When the technology changed, I'd have to learn how to use it, but I had already developed the skills on *how* to learn.

To me, that is the single biggest thing someone can learn from getting an education.

Back to the whole point of learning math that may save your life one day. When my oldest daughter was a freshman in high school, she brought home some math homework. There was one question that they hadn't gone over in class, and she wasn't sure how to do it. She asked for my help.

The question was this: 7 people meet and shake hands; how many handshakes occur? Also, what is the formula for the number of handshakes if the number of people is "n"?

I was stupefied. I seriously sat there for an hour trying to figure it out. No luck. I finally posted the question on Facebook. The answer? nCr = n! / (r! * (n - r)!) Where "n" is the number of people, "r" is the number of people required to do a handshake (in this case "2") and the big letter "C" there means constant or something else that makes it really confusing.

What the heck is "n!"? I must have learned that at some point in time, but I didn't remember—because I don't use it. I told my daughter to see what answer the teacher wanted once they went over the assignment. The teacher's answer? "Oh! I didn't expect any of you to get the answer because I haven't taught you how to do it yet."

Timely Graduation

When I attended BYU, there was a great concern over something called "timely graduation." What does that mean? Well, that it was taking too long for students to graduate. The school identified students who were taking too long and invited them to come to one-on-one meetings with an advisor to review what could be done. (In other words, "inspiring" them to hurry up.)

I dare say a good number of people change their majors at least once while they are in college, hence the reason it took longer. My wife switched. Several of my friends and family members switched. I switched as well.

I won a scholarship for my work in electronics while I was in high school. I took a year of classes at a two year college in electrical engineering. What did I discover? I didn't enjoy it.

I went on my LDS mission, and when I came back, I decided to finish my Associates Degree and then transfer to BYU.

When I started attending BYU, I chose Communications—Broadcasting with an emphasis on Production. Why? When I was in high school, I used my electronics knowledge to become one of the engineers at our radio station, KOHS. While doing that, I got to learn how to edit music, promos and the like—and I thought it was fun.

However, to get into the program at BYU, I was required to take a number of pre-requisites before I could even start to take the classes I wanted to take. By this point in time, considering the credits I had earned at the other school, I was a junior before I was even *in* the program.

In addition, we were required to take a zero credit class four times while in school. It was a one hour a week lecture where we got graded for showing up. It was only offered during the fall and winter, so that was a minimum of two years right there you would have to attend the school.

After I got accepted into the program, we as students were told that the number of credits required for us to graduate with our degree was too high and couldn't realistically be done in four years. Aside from all the communications classes, we were also required to take a boatload of English classes. I had to take so many, in fact, that I realized I only needed to take an additional two English classes to get my minor—which I did.

How did the school resolve the issue of too many credit hours being required? Simple. They took all of the communications classes and reduced the number of credit hours they were worth by 1. In other words, the number of classes didn't change—just how many credits they were worth.

And the biggest irony of all? The one class I spent the most time and effort on was one of my required directing classes. I had to direct several programs, including an interview, a dramatic scene, a musical number, and a few others. In fact, I spent more time on that one class than all of my other classes combined for that semester. Guess how many credits it was worth? That's right: one.

A New Form of Slavery?

I once had a chance to study the Fair Labor Standards Act (or FLSA as it is commonly called). Here is a quote from the FLSA.com web page:

"The FLSA (Fair Labor Standards Act) is the Federal law, sometimes called the overtime law, which insures that wages are paid for all hours worked and that all overtime hours, overtime pay, and collected unpaid overtime due is paid to wage earners."

Like most laws, there are many different aspects to it. I won't bore you with the details, though I will give a few examples.

Let's say you live 5 miles from where you work. Let's also say that it takes you 10 minutes to get there.

Now, to make things interesting, you are assigned to go to a training class which is 55 miles away, and it will take you an hour and a half to get there.

As I understand the law, you would have to get paid whatever time it takes you to get there, minus the time it normally takes you to get to work. So in this example, it would be 90 minutes, minus 10, equaling 80 minutes. Yes, you would be paid 80 minutes of travel time.

For the mileage? It's the same concept: you would be paid for the miles you travel to get to the training (55) minus the normal miles (5) for a total of 50 miles. Most companies pay a set rate per mile for employees when using their own car.

And that's not all. If you work more than 40 hours in a week, you have to get paid overtime for that week. You can't shave off the time the following week, even if it is in the same pay period, to make up the difference.

The government is serious about these rules. When I worked at a certain grocery store in college, a memo was sent out that workers had to be assigned more work than they could do during their shifts so that they would stay busy, but no one was allowed to get overtime. So many of the workers, fearing they would get in trouble, would clock out when their shift was done, but would stay to finish their work, off the clock. This made the press later, and a lawsuit was filed. I was contacted to see how much time I worked off the clock, so I could get part of the settlement. How much did I get? None. You see, I refused to work off the clock. I didn't think it was ethical—though sometimes I would get in trouble for not finishing all my work.

And then there was the shift manager at a certain fast food restaurant I worked at in high school. His method of "encouraging" the employees to finish for the night was to clock them out when their shift should have been done and then have them work on their own time until the job was done. He tried that exactly once on me—a night when someone had called in sick and we were understaffed. The moment he clocked me out, I dropped the broom on the ground, took off my apron, and left the building. The next day when I came to work, the store manager and general manager wanted to talk to me.

Long story, short: that shift manager never clocked people out again.

There is one major exception to the FLSA. It is a term I've come to hate. It is "exempt employee"—meaning you don't get paid by the hour, but rather, you get paid a salary. All those FLSA rules don't apply to exempt employees—and many employers know this and abuse it.

I've heard on more than one occasion that once you become "exempt," the company basically owns you. They can make you work as many hours as they want—demand that you are on call 24/7, and there is nothing you can do about it—unless you quit, and who in their right mind would quit a job when 1 out of 10 people are out of work?

Is it just me, or does being an exempt employee sound a lot like a form of slavery?

Spin

I once saw a headline that said, "Seinfeld actor shoots himself in the head."

Right away, that grabbed my attention.

We would air re-runs of Seinfeld after our 10 o'clock news when I worked in Idaho, so I'd seen all the episodes several times. Who had shot themselves? Was it Jerry? Kramer? George? As it turns out, it was an actor named Daniel von Bargen who played a character named Mr. Kruger. This is a tragic story, but it wouldn't have gotten nearly the interest if the headline had read, "Daniel von Bargen shoots himself in the head."

Daniel von Bargen has eighty-four acting credits to his name (according to IMDB.com), so why include the "Seinfeld" reference in the headline? Because it was a very popular show and I'm sure it resulted in many people (including me) clicking on the link to find out which actor had done it.

This is just an example of "spin"—meaning to take the facts and present them in a way that can bias a person's understanding of the situation. This is very rampant in politics, but it can be found everywhere.

I believe we all "spin" things to some degree. It could be telling your parents, "Guess what! I got all A's in my classes except one!" Granted, that "except one" was an F, but alas, that isn't where we put the focus.

Or how about, "I did the wash today, sweetheart! I've even folded them and put them away!"

Granted, I washed her favorite white shirt with the colors, so now it's pink. But heck, I did the wash!

I once entered a couple of short stories into a contest called *Parables for Today*. I was excited when they announced that one of my stories made the top twenty-five finalists. Then, a few weeks later, they announced the top five *winners*. I took fourth place, given the official title of "Honorable Mention." However, the way it was announced was that I was one of the "winners." So, naturally, I can (and do) call myself an "award-winning author." Is it spin? Yeah, it probably is.

My bio also states I'm an award-winning TV director. That is also true. While at BYU in a highly competitive program, I was awarded the "Silver Microphone" (the highest honor) for directing. Is it a valid award? Yes, very much so. Can people interpret "award-winning TV director" as something else? I'm sure they can. It doesn't mean my bio is untrue.

There are even programs out there for authors on how to become a "bestselling author." What's the spin? Simple. It's a massive blitz to sell enough copies of your book to break the top one hundred of some list. Even if the book is there for only a week, you're still a bestselling author.

So, is "spinning" something the same as telling a lie? Or is it just focusing on a certain part of the truth?

The Right to Choose Actions, Not Consequences

The 4th of July in the United States of America is called Independence Day. It marks the day when the leaders of the young country stood up and basically said, "We are tired of being told what we can and cannot do."

People wanted to be able to worship what they wanted: freedom of religion. People wanted to be able to speak up when their leaders were doing something wrong: freedom of speech. People wanted to be treated fairly: All men are created equal.

It's my belief that the basic concept of freedom is having the right to choose. And I also believe that every person on the earth has this right and ability. What we *don't* have is the right and ability to select the consequences of our actions.

If you stick your hand in a fire, that is your choice. The consequence? You will get burned.

If you don't eat or drink, that is your choice. The consequence? You will get hungry and thirsty.

Too often people confuse the right to choose their actions with a right to choose their consequences.

I had an employee once tell me, "I won't be coming in to work today. It's too snowy outside." While in some lines of work and areas of the country that is acceptable, and actually a good idea, when you work at a 24-hour news station in New England, that doesn't fly. The employee couldn't understand when they were written up for not coming to work—though the expectation was made very clear when they were hired. They said they had the right to choose not to come to work—and I agreed. What they didn't have was the right to choose the consequence for not coming to work.

In my professional life, I've often gotten in trouble for speaking my mind on certain subjects (shocking!)—even though I was sure I was right.

My first job was at a fast food restaurant. When working in the cooking area, we were required to wear hats. However, when the managers came back to help, they never wore hats. When working on a cash drawer, we could be short or over only 50 cents by the end of our shift or we would be written up. However, when we went on break, a manager would take over our drawer. In one of our staff meetings, I brought up these two points—especially about the cash drawer. "If I am held accountable for the money in my drawer, then I should be the only one with access to it." The answer? "Managers are managers because they don't steal and don't make money changing mistakes."

On my last review there, I got a very low rating for having a poor attitude. I can imagine that if the founding fathers of the USA were given a review by the king of England after they declared their independence, their rating would have been similar.

CYA

In the jobs I've had over the years, I've found that I've needed to keep a file simply named "CYA."

Now what does this mean? Well, one way you could phrase it is "Cover Your Assets." It's a file where I would put things to prove this or that in case it came back to bite me later.

Why would I even need such a file? Sadly, it seems that more and more people are doing whatever they can to get ahead—and one really bad way they do it is by tearing other people down.

On more than one occasion, I've had to defend myself against allegations that were nothing more than people trying to make me look bad so that they themselves looked better.

I've seen a growing trend where people are being ranked against their peers—and it's all about being number one.

At one place I worked, a report was sent out daily. It was called "The Motivation Report." It tracked several different categories and then ranked you with an overall score. To make things even more motivational, it would highlight the areas you were doing well in by coloring them green. And if you weren't doing well? It would be in red. And this report was sent to everyone.

There is a fundamental flaw in this process. There can only be one first place winner. So really, how motivational is it to be shown every day that you aren't number one? Again, some people believe the only way to get to the top isn't to excel at their job, but rather, to bring others down, thereby lifting up their ranking.

I've personally seen people do unethical things to increase their ranking, because that was where the focus was. Oh, they might not out and out lie, but they withhold information, or perhaps present the best case as the norm.

I believe this is more widespread than just the workplace. I consider myself to be a fairly intelligent person." I can generally sense when people are trying to pull a fast one on me.

An example? How about those misleading checks you get in the mail? At first glance, they look like a real check. They are written out to me for some usually high dollar amount. Then in small printing, it is written, *"This is not an actual check. By signing and depositing this check, you agree to enroll in some program you really don't need that actually costs four times as much as this check is worth every month. Go ahead and try to contact us. We're available from 5:00 am to 5:15 am Zimbabwe time."*

If you are one of those people who feel you have to be number one, I give you this challenge. Go to a graveyard and find a tombstone that states, "Husband, Father, and Ranked Number 1 in June, August and November of 1973."

The Formula

What people enjoy reading is highly subjective. Some people enjoy reading books that are very descriptive about the setting. Others enjoy character-driven stories, while others focus on the plot. And then there are those who read a book as if it were an essay submitted to a college professor for grading. That's all good, and I'm not going to judge anyone for what they enjoy reading.

To that end, a lot of advice I've received given from other authors focuses around some or all of the different aspects I noted above. Based on the reviews of my books, and including my own preferences in what I read and write, I'd say my style is more character and plot driven. Setting is in the background—admittedly, perhaps too much at times. Technically speaking, that is my weakest area. Thank goodness for excellent editors!

I've run across a few articles and books outlining how a novel should be written for it to be successful. By this, I mean that these reference materials break down at what point during the book you should do this or that. (Examples: introducing a conflict, adding a twist, introducing a new character, and so forth.) In one case, the writer of the article actually referred to it as "the formula."

When I was learning to become a TV newscast director at BYU, we would have guest speakers from various fields come to talk to us. I recall one news director of a local TV station relate this story:

"When I took over as the news director, our station was last place in ratings. I asked the people who worked there why they thought that was the case. They didn't know. One person spoke up and said, 'I don't understand it. We watch other newscasts and we're doing everything they are doing.' You see, that was the problem. It's not enough to do what everyone else is doing. You need to do something *different* to stand out and be successful."

A comment I hear over and over about my books is that they are different from what people expected, and that they don't seem to follow "the formula." My response? GOOD! I wrote them knowing they were different. In the end, the reviews have been overwhelmingly positive.

For those of you who have ever wanted to write a book, may I humbly suggest that you learn all you can from other authors, but in the end, write your own story.

Don't follow "the formula." Don't be predictable; do the unexpected. Only then will you truly stand out among your peers.

Equality For All

"We have bonded."

The wise one looked back and forth between the two young Coyseti. "I do not understand."

"We have bonded," the tall Green Coyseti said. Next to it was another Green Coyseti.

"That is not possible," the wise one said.

The second Green Coyseti spoke. "It is possible. It has happened."

"Greens can only bond to Blues," the wise one said. "It is the only way."

The first Green stepped forward. "It is remarkable, I know. But it is true."

"But new Coyseti can be created only when a Green and a Blue link," the wise one pointed out. "And Coyseti can only link once they have bonded."

The second Green said, "Do the Coyseti believe in equality?"

"Yes."

"Are the Coyseti an enlightened species?"

"Yes."

"Then who is to say two Greens cannot bond?"

The wise one had no answer for this. A bonding was something between two Coyseti. It could not be proved scientifically. When two Coyseti bonded, they knew it, and no one doubted it as long as both of the Coyseti agreed.

"It is not rational," the wise one finally said.

"Bonding is not rational," the first Green said. "When it happens, it happens."

The wise one frowned. "I must confer with my superior."

"Do what you must," the second Green said. "But we are going to tell the Coyseti we have bonded."

Word spread of the two Greens bonding. When two Coyseti bonded, they were granted recognition from the leaders as a bonded pair. The two Greens were *not* recognized, despite their claim of bonding. The situation eventually came to the leader of the Coyseti's attention.

"What do the Coyseti want?" the leader asked his council.

"It is unclear," one of them answered, an older Green. "Some say we should not allow it. They say it is unnatural."

A younger Blue spoke up. "But others say it is not for us to judge. We are a society built on equality for all. They claim that we are putting restrictions on that equality."

The leader of the Coyseti frowned. "Which of the groups is the most vocal?"

"As of now, both sides have supporters. But there is a group called 'Equality for All' which is growing in popularity. They support unrestricted recognitions of bondings."

After thinking a moment, the leader decided, "We shall wait and see which group gains the most supporters."

౿

Equality for All, or EFA as they were called, grew in numbers. Their slogan was "Equality Without Restrictions!"

Some Coyseti wore garments with the slogan, while others displayed signs. And at every meeting of the wise ones or the council, the slogan was chanted by the members of the EFA.

Those Coyseti that believed bonding should only be between Greens and Blues called themselves "Traditionalists." They claimed the EFA's views were offensive and unnatural.

Some of the EFA said it was fear or hatred that kept the Traditionalists from supporting their cause.

At last, the leader of the Coyseti made a decision. It read, "After listening to the Coyseti and advice from the wise ones and my council, I have decided to support Equality for All. From this day forward, any two Coyseti that have declared that they have bonded will be officially recognized."

The EFA celebrated. The Traditionalists mourned.

❧

"We have bonded."

The wise one looked back and forth between the two Coyseti. "I do not understand."

"We have bonded," the old Green Coyseti said. Next to it was a young Blue Coyseti, still in its primary years.

"That is not possible," the wise one said. "The Blue is too young."

The Blue Coyseti spoke. "It is possible. It has happened. And the law states equality without restrictions."

❧

"We have bonded."

The wise one looked back and forth between the two Coyseti. "I do not understand."

"We have bonded," the Green Coyseti said. Next to it was a Blue Coyseti.

"That is not possible," the wise one said. "The Blue is already bonded to someone else."

The Blue Coyseti spoke. "It is possible. It has happened. And the law states equality without restrictions."

❧

"We have bonded."

The wise one looked back and forth between the two Coyseti. "I do not understand."

"We have bonded," the Green Coyseti said. Next to it was a Blue Coyseti.

"That is not possible," the wise one said. "You come from the same bonded pair."

The Blue Coyseti spoke. "It is possible. It has happened. And the law states equality without restrictions."

❧

Word of these different types of bondings rippled through the Coyseti.

Many argued that these Coyseti didn't understand the law and used it to create bondings that were offensive and unnatural. Some of the most vocal in their criticism were the founders of the EFA.

Restaurants

Jim entered the restaurant and noticed everyone was looking at him. Their expressions showed different emotions: anticipation, curiosity, indifference, and disdain. Everyone was in either a fancy dress or a tuxedo. He looked down at his T-shirt and blue jeans. They were clean and free of holes or rips, yet still he felt uncomfortable.

He had heard good things about this restaurant. The food was supposed to be excellent. He hadn't realized how the patrons would be dressed.

"Welcome," the hostess said. She smiled at him. "How many?"

He'd come by himself, which only added to his feeling of awkwardness. The food smelled delicious and his mouth started to water.

Still, his growing feeling of uneasiness overrode his desire to eat.

"Sorry," he mumbled. "I must have come to the wrong place."

He spun and left the restaurant then walked out to the busy street. Everywhere he looked, he saw different restaurants.

People were walking up and down the sidewalks, looking at the different places to eat.

Jim saw several people wearing T-shirts and blue jeans going into a restaurant a bit further down the street. He followed after them.

He stepped into the restaurant. No one looked up at him when he came in. There wasn't a hostess at the door to greet him. He saw that he would have to go up to the counter and place his order and then find a place to sit.

The menu was on the wall lit up with neon lights. Most of the meals listed were offered at the restaurants he'd visited before.

Jim walked up to the counter, placed his order, and soon was sitting down to eat.

"I'm so glad I left that fancy restaurant across the street," someone said at a table next to him. "I didn't like all the way they ran it."

"Yeah," another person said. "While most of the people were nice, I felt like some of them judged me because I didn't wear a tuxedo."

"And they didn't have my favorite drink!" yet another person said. "I tried to get them to offer it, but they wouldn't. They are so close minded."

Jim looked around the restaurant. In general, people were eating and looked comfortable.

His meal was okay, but he thought back to how the food smelled at the nicer restaurant. He wondered how that would have tasted.

Equals

I parked my well-worn Datsun between a BMW and a Jaguar. When the students in my girlfriend's apartment complex noticed my car, they did so with perplexed expressions.

Arching my back and extending my hands forward, I stretched my arms which ached from grinding meat all morning. I hated that in order to get time off on Saturday I had to work until midnight on Friday and then five to eleven on Saturday mornings. The meat department bored me, but it paid the bills.

I checked my forehead in the rearview mirror to make sure the zit I'd popped that morning hadn't come back with friends. Convinced I looked good, I got out of the car.

It was a little before noon. The October sky was bright blue with just a few clouds swimming along at a leisurely pace. Red, orange and yellow leaves made the mountains seem as if they were on fire. It should be a nice day for a picnic.

I approached Becky's apartment. She was cute and fun. That's what I needed in my life right now. Becky claimed to be five three—but I think she measured herself wearing high heels. When we said goodnight, she would stand on the bottom step of her front porch stairs. She liked that it made us "equals" as she called it. I thought that was weird, but it made it easier to kiss her.

Her apartment had a doorbell, something of a novelty. I rang once, and then again. A moment later, Sabrina, Becky's roommate, opened the door and squinted into the sunlight.

"Adam? What are you doing here?" she asked.

"Picking up Becky. Guess she didn't tell you."

Sabrina shook her head. "She's still asleep. Are you sure you have the right time?"

My watch read noon on the dot. "Yeah. Guess she forgot to set her alarm—again."

"Come in." Sabrina opened the door. She held an embroidered terrycloth robe closely around her.

When I entered, I noticed the curtains were all drawn and the lights were off.

"Oh, I'm sorry. Did I wake you, Sabrina?"

"Nah, I was watching TV in my bedroom. Have a seat. I'll check on Beck."

Sabrina left the main room and headed down a hallway. She was nice enough, if a little dense. Then again, Becky wasn't exactly a scholar either.

I feigned interest in the room's only painting while I waited. It featured a sun setting over an ocean, and it looked expensive.

"Adam?" Becky said groggily when she came into the room. "Wow, I'm sorry. I overslept."

"It's okay." It really wasn't, but I didn't want to fight. "Are you sick?"

"I'm fine. Just tired."

"Oh… Do you want to cancel the picnic?"

"No, no." She took a half-step forward and then regained her balance. "I just need a few minutes to get ready. Okay?"

"Okay."

She turned and stumbled her way down the hallway. A moment later, I heard the shower turn on.

I ran my fingers through my hair, fighting the urge to be upset. I didn't have a lot of free time and Becky didn't seem to understand that—though I'd explained it to her on several occasions. I tried to distract myself by looking around their main room— my whole apartment could fit in it. There were three couches, two recliners and a big screen TV.

Sabrina came back into the room. Becky's roommate had changed into some capris and a loose fitting blouse. She was cute, but not really my type. I liked short blondes, like Becky. And Becky liked tall guys, like me.

"It's going to be a nice day," Sabrina said.

"I hope so. We're going on a picnic."

Sabrina sighed. "Ah, that's romantic. I wish Brian would do stuff like that with me."

I noticed Sabrina had several new hickies since I'd seen her last. "Have you asked him?"

She laughed. "Yeah, right." Sabrina sat across from me in one of the recliners. "How's school going?" she asked.

"Good. Busy. I'm taking fourteen credits."

"Fourteen? Wow. I'm only taking eight and that's killing me. Beck doesn't even have that many."

"Yeah, she's taking six."

Sabrina twirled her long, dark hair in her fingers. "She's always complaining about biology. Good thing you're helping her."

Becky and I met in an English class during the summer term. I'd agreed to take biology with her—a class I needed anyway—because she was nervous she wouldn't pass it without help.

"Yeah, well, I do my best." I stretched out my arms and heard my elbows pop. The sound caught Sabrina's attention.

"Has anyone told you you've got Popeye-like forearms?" she asked.

I smiled. "Yeah. Benefit from my job."

"You work as well as go to school, right?"

"Yup."

"Why are you working so hard?" she asked.

I bit off my reply that not everyone had their parents pay for school and living expenses. Instead, I answered, "Because it will pay off in the end."

"But how do you know?"

"I have to trust that it will—or there's no point spending the time to do it."

"Huh." She got up. "I was going to make me some breakfast. Want some?"

"No thanks. We'll be picking up KFC soon."

Sabrina looked confused a moment. "Oh yeah. The picnic."

We chatted a few more minutes. She told me Becky's divorced parents had been fighting again and not to bring them up. She asked me about my other classes. I was studying to be an electrical engineer. She asked if that meant I'd learn how light bulbs work and stuff. I nodded.

Becky came into the room. "I'm ready."

Her blonde hair was styled so it just touched her shoulders. She wore cut-off blue jeans and a tight, white shirt that showed off her figure. My pulse quickened when I saw her.

"You look hot," I said.

She tried to smile, but it turned into a yawn. "Sorry, I'm still a little tired I guess."

I stood. "It's okay. We'll have the picnic and if you're still feeling tired, we can cut the date short."

"I'll be fine."

"Beck," Sabrina said, "you shouldn't feel bad if you come home early. After all, it's Adam's fault you're so tired."

"My fault?"

I saw Becky glaring at her roommate and shaking her head, but Sabrina didn't notice.

"Yeah," Sabrina said, "he kept you up too late last night. It was like what—after three when you came home?"

I looked at Becky and she glanced at me. She looked scared.

"Sabrina," I said, "I wasn't with Becky."

"Oh? Then who took you out?" she asked her roommate.

"Yes, Becky, who took you out?" I echoed. I knew I sounded angry and I didn't care.

She went to the front door, opened it and said, "I'll talk to you *later*, Brina."

I followed her out the door. She walked down the stairs and headed toward the parking lot. I stopped at the bottom of the stairs and sat on the lowest step.

When she realized I hadn't followed her, she turned around. I motioned for her to sit by me. I could tell she didn't want to, but she also knew I could be stubborn.

She sat on the step, but as far away from me as possible.

"Something you want to tell me?" I asked.

"No."

"Let me rephrase that," I said. "Is there something you *should* tell me?"

"You'll just get madder."

"Why would I get madder? Oh, yeah. Let's see. My girlfriend went on a date with some other guy last night. I think that's a pretty good reason."

"It wasn't a date."

"What do you mean it wasn't—"

She interrupted me. "A friend from high school came into town yesterday. We keep in touch. He said he wanted to catch up and offered to take me to dinner. You were working and I didn't have other plans. So, we went to dinner—that's all."

I folded my arms across my chest. "Dinner until three in the morning?"

"No, we didn't eat until three in the morning." She sounded defensive.

"Then what *did* you do?"

"He drove me back here. We sat in his car and talked. Time got away from me is all. We didn't kiss or anything." She turned toward me. "You shouldn't be mad. I didn't do anything wrong."

"Becky, we've been dating for five months. *You* were the one who wanted to date each other exclusively."

"I know! And that's why I told Robbie I wouldn't kiss him."

"He tried?"

"Of course! We dated in high school."

I stared at her in disbelief.

"What?" she asked.

"What do you mean *what*?"

"See! I knew you'd get mad. That's why I wasn't going to tell you."

I took in a deep breath. When I exhaled I didn't feel angry anymore, I felt something different. Sadness.

"Oh, Becky…" I hung my head and shook it. I had too much going on in my life to deal with this kind of drama. Looking forward to dates with Becky was supposed to be the thing that got me through the week.

I think the change of my tone scared her more than me being mad. Her eyes grew wide and her countenance changed.

"Adam? No! Don't do it. I didn't do anything wrong." Her words were mangled with sobs. "You can't break up with me! I need you!"

"I'm not breaking up with you."

I stood up from the step. I looked at her. "*You* broke up with *me*."

"But I didn't! I didn't! He wanted to kiss me, but I stopped him."

"It would have been easier if you *had* kissed him," I said. "At least then I think you'd get it."

"Get what?"

Mascara was running down her cheeks.

"Trust." I paused to see if she understood. She didn't. "Good-bye, Becky."

I left her crying on the step. As I returned to my car, I noticed how out of place the BMW and Jaguar looked next to my Datsun.

Double Your Money Back

My wife and I often watch a TV show to wind down the night. Usually we have the shows on DVR so we zip through the commercials, but sometimes we watch them "in real time." Other times we'll mute the TV and make up our own narration to what is on the screen. Or we'll just talk, waiting for the commercials to end.

One night, we had it muted and were talking when a commercial for toilet paper came on. At the end, it offered a "double your money back guarantee." Since we didn't have the sound on, I didn't hear what the conditions were, but it really struck me as funny. Like, laughing so hard tears came to my eyes. (My wife, being the more mature of the two of us, just rolled her eyes at me.)

Think about it: what are you going to have to say or do to prove you aren't happy with toilet paper?

So for curiosity's sake, I decided to look up some products that offered a "double your money back" deal, and what conditions must be met.

These are 100% real. I'm not including the product names so I don't get sued.

"Just use our products for a year. If you don't see any reactions in that time, just contact us for help. Sometimes a little social training is all you need for success. If you still don't see any reactions after

getting help, send the empty bottles back with a note detailing what happened at least 7 times you used them, and we'll give you double your money back."

Wow! If the product doesn't work after a year, they'll give me social training? How could anyone say no to that? And don't get me started on the 7 detailed notes...

"30 Day Double Your Money Back Guarantee. That's obviously a very bold statement. We can make this guarantee because of the faith we have in (our product). (Then the small print): The Guarantee does not guarantee any user will profit as we have no way of knowing if you will follow (our) rules."

So basically, they have faith in their product, but they don't promise you'll actually gain anything from it because you may be doing it wrong.

Heck, that statement doesn't sound so bold anymore, does it?

"If, within 7 days of the date of our report, you provide proof that with the same type of search, and using the same information you gave us to process your order, more current, more complete or more accurate information was obtained legally through any other similar service advertised on the

Internet, we will promptly refund double what you paid us."

I love this one. So, you pay them to do a search for you. And in order to prove they didn't do a good job, you have to pay someone else to do the same job and hope they find better results. AND you only have 7 days to do it.

"We are so confident that (our product) will solve your odor problems that we can offer an unconditional 30-Day Double Your Money Back Guarantee. No other odor remover has a guarantee this strong. If you're less than satisfied with (our product) contact us within 30 days of purchase by calling toll-free 800-XXX-XXXX. We'll work with you to make sure that the product is applied in the best way to eliminate your particular odor problems."

Ah, again. One of those products where if it doesn't work, it's because you, the consumer, are doing it wrong.

"In the rare event of a product failure, you will need to supply (us) with the following:
Original dated store receipt. Product packaging—this means keeping ALL packaging (empty bottles, box, cardboard, etc.) along with your original receipt. Official proof of failure. Request

must be postmarked within 30 days of results. Please allow 4-6 weeks for processing. Failure to supply all required components & documents will void your eligibility to the 200% double money back guarantee."

Notice that they don't really state what they mean by "official proof of failure." I'm surprised they didn't also demand a note from your mother.

After reading all these, I'm inspired to offer a double your money back guarantee on any of my books. It goes as follows:

"If, after reading (insert the name of the book), you are less than satisfied with it, I'll give you double your money back."

Fine print: *You must read the book at least 7 times. If you don't "get" it, have someone read it to you at least twice. If still less than satisfied, buy 15 more books from other authors that are more satisfying. Send the following items to me in order to get double your money back: the original receipt (must be notarized), a list of the 15 books you bought with letters from all of their authors explaining why their books were more satisfying, video proof you actually read the book 7 times, and lastly, send me the book (must be in near mint condition!) so I can sell it to someone else. Allow 4 to 6 decades for processing.*

About the Author

Author J. Lloyd Morgan is an award-winning author and television director. He graduated from Brigham Young University with a degree in Communications and a minor in English.

Morgan has lived all over the United States, but now resides in North Carolina with his wife and four daughters. Aside from writing, Morgan is an avid reader. He's also a huge fan of baseball and enjoys listening to progressive rock.

He is the author of the novels *The Hidden Sun* and *The Waxing Moon*. His published short stories include *Howler King, I Heard the Bells on Christmas Day, The Reluctant Wanderer,* and award-winning *The Doughnut*.

Index